JULIE MYERSON

sleepwalking

PICADOR

First published 1994 by Picador

This edition published 1995 by Picador
an imprint of Macmillan General Books
25 Eccleston Place London SW1W 9NF
and Basingstoke

Associated companies throughout the world

ISBN 0 330 33611 8

5 7 9 8 6 4

A CIP catalogue record for this book is available from
the British Library

Printed and bound in Great Britain by
Mackays of Chatham PLC, Chatham, Kent

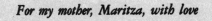

For my mother, Maritza, with love

The epigraphs to each chapter are from 'Barefoot in the Dark' by Professor Jim Horne of Loughborough University of Technology, an article published in the *Guardian* in March 1989, and I am very grateful for his permission to reproduce them.

Ede remarks, shortly after my father dies, that suicide is a death which leaves its traces, and at the time I find the idea almost comforting. Because I think I know exactly what she means.

It's only much later that I realize that I never did – that neither of us knew anything, that his effect was only just beginning. For when you make your own death as he did, you deliberately stir the black silt on the bottom – disturbing all that debris which should be left down there in darkness – and it floats up, half-roused, to wreak its own particular damage.

But I don't have the benefit of this knowledge at the start. What I do have is a feeling of alarm, a hot panic which wakes me up at night, a creeping certainty that something isn't quite right.

In the end I distil it down to a single icy thought: that if he really is dead and gone for ever, then why the hell don't I feel better?

Queenie Hancock had never wanted children. She just wasn't all that keen on them.

'I'm not having kiddies. George knows that – I'm just

not the maternal type,' she told anyone at the Golf Club who cared to listen. But then Nature elbowed her way in and somehow they did make a child and, though she secretly threw herself down the last seven steps of the stairs when she was a few weeks gone, it was no good and she ended up giving birth to Douglas on the drawing-room floor – 'Just like going to the toilet,' she said.

And so suddenly there he was, this ugly little scrap with a weak heart and bandy legs. Somehow a cuckoo in her deft and otherwise perfectly ordered nest.

one

'Even in the deepest of non-dreaming sleep, our thought processes continue. Our ruminations are often dull, sometimes funny, maybe sad. But occasionally, they get out of hand or, to be more precise, get out of bed, and sleepwalk.'

'He's gone, Susan' – her voice cuts in and out, distorted by the car phone – 'I'm sorry, I don't know how you're going to feel. It's going to be a shock, after all this time.'

She calls me on a dark and rainy day – bruised sky, drained of colour by a howling wind, the last of the thin daylight already spiriting itself away. I sit filing photocopied receipts against patients' names, so tired I can hardly alphabeticize. A and E seem interchangeable, a hieroglyphical blur which worsens the familiar nausea already hacking its way through my system, encouraged by the sensation of the baby kicking inside me. 'I'm sorry, darling, but I knew you'd want to know . . . Hold on, I'm pulling into the inside lane.' A click as a cigarette is lit.

I rest my hand on my belly, where my child waits, knees flexed, in safe limbo. I hear low voices as Mr Sudbury treats a patient in the next room. I swallow and my nose begins to run. There's a pause, which seems to contain a struggle. I hear my own breath.

'Mummy, what?'

She continues:

'Apparently your father died yesterday, sometime in the afternoon, in his car . . . I've only just been told . . . they didn't have your names of course, and the solicitor took all this time to track me down . . .'

'A crash?'

There's a click of recognition somewhere in my body, near the cavern of my heart, as I take this idea in. I flex a paper-clip between my fingers, pulling the two thin loops apart, gently teasing. I hear my hard voice, feel my mouth go dry, my tongue touch fur on the insides of my teeth. I see crunched-up metal, shoes flung into the verge, amongst the bracken and the litter. My father's balding head imploded on the steering-wheel. I wonder what I feel.

'No.' Surprisingly, there's a small sob in her voice. And then a hiss, as the phone cuts out again. '. . . the awful bit, I'm afraid . . . the car was in the garage. He gassed himself – you know, carbon monoxide.'

The paper-clip gives, about to snap, but I push it back together again, straighten it, save it, place it against the magnet on the desk. 'Oh,' I say, and then I sneeze.

Mrs Hoffman comes in. We talk about her grapefruit diet, her cystitis, and Prince Rainier of Monaco. His picture is on the front of *Hello!* magazine. 'Look,' she says, tapping the page with stubby pearl-pink nails, 'it's been one tragedy after another for that family, he hasn't smiled since he lost Grace. Some people have such appalling bad luck.'

'Yes,' I say, 'they do,' handing her a crisp turquoise seersucker gown.

'How are you, Sue my love?' asks Mrs Varten, placing a Fox's Glacier Mint from her handbag on my blotter. 'Still with us? Your hubby doesn't mind you working right up to the bitter end, then? I tell you, it was a different story in my day.'

'They're different men these days,' says Mrs Lawson, who's younger than the others. 'Well, aren't they? I expect Susan's husband will change nappies. I expect he'll insist upon it, won't he, dear?'

'I suppose so,' I say, suddenly uncertain of almost everything.

My father was a cruel and pathetic sort of a man, for many years more dead for me than alive, so the idea that his body had finally joined his heart and soul is really neither particularly odd nor tragic. But I find myself remembering, for the first time in years, a macabre recurring dream I had about him all through my adolescence.

In the dream, I'd be somewhere in the air looking down. Next, I'd zoom in on a corner of a windswept field, suffused with a bland, dead light. And there he'd be, just standing there in this corner, a man in a colourless raincoat. Faceless and featureless, but some brute inner wisdom always told me this was him. My badge of steady misery, my Daddy. Frantic, quick, he'd be soaking himself with some liquid from a can. Never looking up, his hands and shoulders moving in a panic-stricken way I couldn't bear to watch. And just as I'd always known it was him, so too I'd know it was paraffin in the can. And as I stared at him from my place in that hushed, empty sky, he'd pull his cigarette lighter from his pocket. And I'd wake just at the precise moment that his whole body burst into flames.

Lurid and quick, the dream always left me hot with shame. I'd know, as I drifted towards sleep, that it was coming, because a certain set of recognizable sensations would wash over me. Textures would change. Ordinary, harmless sounds were magnified. The tick of the alarm clock developed a remorseless beat, the gurgle of the water pipes on the landing was fat with significance. But I had no power to stop myself, and suddenly there I'd be, floating, waiting for it to happen.

As I got older – as I grew up I suppose – the dream came less and less often, though I did still dream it occasionally, and when I did the same vague hangover of shame would stay with me, washing over me in the darkness – almost sexual in the way it could alter my bodily sensations in seconds.

But it is only now that he's finally done it, that I'm struck by the naked, difficult truth. That now that the dream has gone, here in its place is a fact. That some part of me has been predicting, hastening – precipitating? – his death for the best part of my growing-up life.

*

sleepwalking

Sometimes magic is all around us. Sometimes it's clear that our precursors are not in fact gone, but only wrapped around us in distant, subtle layers, binding and constricting us, imprinting themselves upon our limbs like bandages.

Queenie May Sanderson – baptized Victoria but always called Queenie, a pet name, a joke, of her age – was born into a particularly violent electric storm one August night almost a hundred years ago. Her first memory, if she had one, would be of a distant roar of thunder, bright yellow sky, and her own ragged moan as she burst from the shelter of her mother's belly – long splinters of pain flying out to lodge in the Bunter sandstone walls of the dark house. As she was born into that room of sweat and blood and candles, water dripped from every parapet outside, every piece of guttering. She did not know that it had rained all night – a black, hard, insistent rain, every drop of which screamed out that light was still a long way off.

Queenie weighed six pounds. She had no hair and was covered in a warm white paste which they tried to wipe off. She was furious. She yelled and straightened her legs so her whole body was taut and airless.

'Bit of jaundice,' said the nurse, struggling against her, 'but what a strong girl. Do you want to hold her when she's wrapped?' But Vi just turned her head away and wept, as she'd wet the bed and her behind stung, and she couldn't bring herself to tell them.

They gave Queenie a bottle, which she drank greedily.

She didn't bother to cry after that. Slowly, the glass rectangle of window changed colour and dried. Somebody remarked that in Bulwell two people had been killed in the storm.

In the grey relief of morning, Queenie (though no one had yet thought to name her that) lay tightly swaddled in the crib, sallow cheeked and silent, appearing to watch them all. She watched the midwives swishing around with bowls and cloths. She watched her mother, alive and transparent against the pillow. And she watched her father, rigid and unsmiling in a chair by the window – baffled at his lack of a son, and supremely sad and uncomfortable in the presence of so many women.

My father once told me that the most comfortable way in the world to die would be to run a warm bath, then slice a knife into your wrists and literally let the life gush out of you.

'Very easy, almost pleasant,' he smiled, sucking on a slim cigar. I was nine and I pictured a cheese knife sliding into flesh, snagging veins, and the skin from my chin to my breastbone goosepimpled, and I know he enjoyed it. I saw slicks of blood lapping against the showerhead, a greasy haemoglobin tide mark. Every suggestion of his took root in my brain, and he knew it. Yet I also knew he'd panic if cornered, and he knew I knew, and held it against me, threatening me with it now and then as cowards do. I thought all fathers were like that.

sleepwalking

All the same it seems surprising now, as I walk down Seymour Street towards the tube. 'You mustn't blame yourself, Susan,' my mother had insisted an hour earlier, but even as she spoke I saw his face, vindictive, taut with accusation. I buy my ticket, drop my change on to the soiled mauve plush of an open guitar case, and move in a rush of dirty wind down the escalator.

My belly shudders as I sit on the bench and gaze at the ground. His first, unborn grandchild. I pull my coat around me and slide my hand under my jumper, touching the flesh which is so full and hard, feeling what must be the heel of a little foot moving under my fingers.

'Not long to go, eh? When's the big day?' A tall woman stands in front of me. Her long grey hair is tied with string and she carries a wrinkled copy of *Time* magazine. Her white Reeboks have been painted purple with shoe-dye, and her skin has the strange and unattractive smoothness of the fanatically religious. She could, all the same, pass for an academic or teacher, except for the sharp and betraying smell of piss coming from her skirts. I give a weak, dismissive smile.

'Oh, a while,' I say. I've learned not to be any more specific than that. Christmas Day is far too colourful, too inviting. To be quite visibly hatching a baby under your coat is bad enough – owning up to Christmas Day is just asking for it. My train comes and I sink gratefully into my seat. The grey-haired woman sits down opposite, watching me whenever I catch her eye, with an unpleasantly intimate smile. I stare right over her head.

9

Julie Myerson

Fifteen minutes later, when I get out at Clapham
Common, I glance back to see that she's still grinning at
me. Her lips are unpleasantly full, her teeth jagged and
sharp. I forget her the moment I step on to the street, but
a few days later, doing something quite haphazard and
irrelevant, I remember her with a sudden melting terror as
if she were a premonition of something unspeakably bad.

I met my husband at a precarious time – a time when I
was bound to meet someone or other, a time when
I stumbled through life like a sleepwalker, waiting to be
woken and found out.

I was twenty-seven.

It was a long summer, the hottest for years, and I was
ill and exhausted. I'd been out of art school a year, with
still no permanent job in sight and massively in debt. I
couldn't go to my mother for help. She knew I had an
overdraft, but she had no idea of its actual size. And anyway,
she would have summoned me home, and I was determined
to stay on in London and somehow continue to paint. In
the spring, I'd sold two paintings, and this sudden burst
of success had sustained me for months. The money had
paid an overdue electricity bill, but the phone had meanwhile been cut off, and I lived off cottage cheese and
crackers.

I'd been selling shirts all through July and August to
anyone foolish enough to remain in the city. I'd climb
stairs, ride airless lifts, up to air-conditioned offices, shiver-

ing whilst men in sweaty stripes sifted through more of the same. One hundred per cent cotton lawn with button-down collars. I got used to the routine. They flirted and showed off, giving the impression they might buy, but it was in fact very hard to make a sale. I was no more than an amusing tea-break to them.

Early one afternoon I went into a management consultancy on the seventh floor of a block near St Paul's. I noticed Alistair straight away as the tallest and most polished of the men. The boss, I thought. Though easy and laughing with the rest of them, he sat slightly apart, perched on a desk, his feet on a swivel chair, trousers hitched up to reveal surprisingly schoolboyish grey socks. He didn't look at the shirts, but sat, swilling the dregs around in his polystyrene coffee cup, and then he folded his arms and put his head on one side and looked at me hard. He had to squint because of the sunshine – it was another bright, hot afternoon. Through the huge window, the cathedral made an unlikely backdrop for his face. Somehow it suited him, lent him a notable grace. The sun rippled through the glass, lit the city. Buildings floated and swayed in the heat.

It was very sudden. I'd had no breakfast or lunch, my head ached and my throat was on fire. 'You look like you could do with a sandwich,' he said.

'Oh no,' I said quickly, not sure whether he was actually offering me one or not. 'Well, I've got so many calls.' He smiled at me for what felt like too long. I mustn't give out the wrong signals, I thought, he's not my type. And then it was too late because I fell to the floor in a dead faint.

I still don't remember how I started seeing him – how this pitiful scene with the faint and the coffee dregs turned into dinner and then more. The doctor diagnosed a bad case of glandular fever, and I know that Alistair drove me to the hospital for my second blood test and I can't have known him more than a few days by that time. He just took charge, and I remember being somewhat in awe of this.

I later discovered it was his trademark. Comfort and strength radiated from Alistair like a kind of happiness. People were drawn to it, to him. You could actually see it happening. At parties, they listened and laughed and leaned forward to touch parts of his body – a knuckle, an elbow, a shoulder, his jaw if only they'd dared – as if they might go away from him lit up in some way. He was beautiful and unthreatening as a piece of good architecture. You wanted to stand a little way away and stare. Briefly, I fell in love with what others saw in him. I knew my bedsit days were over.

'Well, what a lovely man,' my mother congratulated me only a month later as he sprinted up the stairs of her house to wash his large clean hands. 'Now he's the one I'd marry if I were you.' She flicked on the Magimix and checked her make up in the small mirror she kept in the kitchen for that purpose. 'Anyone can see he really cares about you.'

I knew they'd hit it off. After dinner she poured him a whisky and put on her Patsy Cline records. Her husband

— my stepfather — had left her the previous winter, and she was glad of new company. I was more tired and sober than they. Alistair laid his arms on my shoulders. 'Sweetheart, you're exhausted, go to bed,' he said.

I obeyed and they stayed up late together drinking and laughing and playing chess, a pair of grown-ups. Both were doing it for me, of course. And I suppose I knew then, as I lingered in my mother's bedroom, buffing my nails and testing her expensive creams, that he would be her son-in-law. I fell asleep in my old single bed, sober, cleansed and relieved.

Back in London the following night, we had a take-away and made love on the grey, unyielding futon at his flat in a suddenly dark and accomplished way, like two people with something to prove. The next night — as if meeting my mother had somehow clinched it — he asked me to marry him. It was barely six weeks since I'd passed out on his office floor.

I blushed. I was pretty fed up, depressed even. Here was a little piece of life, come out of the blue to rescue me. 'Yes,' I said, faintly shocked at myself for not thinking at all, 'yes, OK.' We were in a tandoori in Stockwell, empty except for the waiters who circled the tables in their dark suits. I wondered whether he'd been joking and was suddenly overcome with embarrassment. I picked furiously at the plastic backing on the menu with my nails. But he looked warm and delighted and didn't seem to notice. I thought about getting up and running like hell.

Then I laughed, and he laughed back and I glanced into his eyes, and saw nothing in particular there.

At his insistence, I gave up selling shirts whilst I recovered from my illness in his tiny, immaculate flat in Battersea. Every evening, he made an effort to come home by seven, and he'd kiss me for some time on the sofa with warm, wet lips, and then we'd go out to dinner somewhere nearby, lingering, arm in arm, in the leafy streets, enjoying the end of the summer, the dying heat.

When I was better, I got my job at the clinic, as receptionist and secretary to three osteopaths. In a funny way, boring though it might have seemed to anyone else, I loved it from the start. It was easy work – undemanding and well paid, and it left my brain blank and thirsty. I always arrived home with a fantastic urge to scatter colour on canvas. Not that Alistair cared much whether or not I did that. He couldn't get excited about art – couldn't see any point in that, the only thing I cared about – but he didn't oppose it either and, in the early days, that was all that mattered. I was very happy. It was amazing and novel to belong to someone – I got a genuine kick out of it. Sex with Alistair was careful and thorough – as if, for the first time, it had been done properly. When he explored my body, it was overwhelming, suffocating. I fell asleep long after him, hypnotized, finally, by the sound of his even, certain breathing.

It's true, if I'm honest, that the first year was good and happy, companionable. We swapped Alistair's clean, compact flat for a whole house in Clapham – late Victorian, with a shiny black front door and privet hedge and, most importantly, a converted loft for me to paint in. Four small children had lived in the house and for the first few weeks their energy seemed to ricochet around it, almost tangible, as if the front door had only just closed on the last of them. We kept finding stubs of wax crayons and small dusty socks in kitchen drawers and behind radiators. Though we never said, I think Alistair and I found it romantic – this coy and constant reference to children, hinting at our own potential for procreation, our own future together. We even discussed it once or twice.

'What about it?' he said one day when we'd been married no time at all, coming up behind me and locking his fingers over mine.

'I don't know,' I said, uncertain, laughing, 'give me a moment or two. Let me get used to all this.'

For a day or so after that, I felt inexplicably depressed.

I meant it. It was different for him, things had scarcely changed. He'd simply planted me in his life. Though we'd left his actual flat, the shell, behind, it was all the same his life that we'd transplanted to the house in Clapham. All his habits, his trimmings, collected on ten years of a high income: his steely grey bachelor sheets from Heals, his Whittards coffee, his *Financial Times* delivered in the morning, the crime thrillers he read in the bath, the order in which he liked to do things, I adopted it all very willingly because it seemed so civilized. I mean, it was all his, but I basked in the sheer comfort of it. I'd come a long, long way from my bedsit and no breakfast and trudging the city with my holdall of shirts. Some adjusting was necessary.

Make no mistake, I was glad. I entered into the spirit of things and groomed myself for wifehood. I had the ragged ends of my hair chopped off, so it just brushed my shoulders, sleek and heavy, and I threw out all of my limp, bedsit underwear that was dyed pink or grey in scummy launderettes. I washed sweaters by hand, and dried them flat, on towels spread in the large airing cupboard. I bought a salad spinner and made dressings using expensive oil, grilled fish with slices of lemon wedged in the pale cold flesh, making sure to clean the grill pan straight afterwards. In fact, I cleaned everything straight afterwards; the only smells in my house were of Domestos and Mr Sheen, and the faint, expensive whiff of Alistair's aftershave as he passed through our dark, shiny hall and out to work. There was a certain easy satisfaction to be had from acting so impeccably.

Of course, despite the loft where I'd planted my easel and a kettle, I didn't manage to paint quite so much, but I told myself I would catch up later. This was a rare honeymoon period (we'd had to postpone our actual honeymoon somewhat indefinitely because of Alistair's work), and we both knew it wouldn't come again. We had conversations. Glasses of good wine over supper. Quickly, we developed our own in-jokes. We saw friends sometimes, but were equally happy alone. Flesh responded to flesh. Alistair stroked my knees and pushed his hands inside my shirt when we watched TV, rolling my nipples between his finger and thumb like Plasticine. He was my husband; there were still things to find out.

I believed I was happy for some time but then, early in the second year, something broke, there was a damage – at least in my perception of our relationship. I can't remember when I first noticed it, on which actual day or morning or moment my marriage suddenly looked different to me, but something vital shifted, there was a subtle gear-change, and we just weren't in step.

We didn't disagree about anything in particular; I don't think we even had rows. There just wasn't anything left to share – no real reason, in fact, to be together. A slow, irritable tension set in. We waited for one another to finish speaking. Or did not speak (or listen) at all. Whatever tenderness there was, was gradually replaced by routine, and we meandered from one moment to the next, expecting that the simple fact of our marriage would tell us what to do. Alistair stayed at the office later and later, arriving home tired and smelling of Indian restaurants. Then I'd come down from the loft to find him watching TV with a glazed expression, though he always smiled and patted the sofa to make me sit down. Oh, he was good to me still, but the harder he appeared to try, the worse it became.

I think he knew it was me. He hadn't changed. He was still the man I'd married. He was one of those men who deserved to have a wife – the sort of man who really did bring home flowers (anaemic, forced chrysanthemums, wrapped tightly in polythene, their stems dark and sloppy from having stood too long in water outside tube stations and delicatessens, but, all the same – flowers) for his wife.

Anyone could see, he had blossomed in his married state. His friends insisted that he was a changed man, that they'd never believed he'd settle down, and that he'd softened somehow, relaxed, his edges blurred by domesticity. He'd only needed a wife, to make him happy, they said. But it wasn't a comfort, I didn't care: everything he did maddened me. As he relaxed, I suffocated.

He woke early and brought me tea which I forgot to drink and left to go cold by the bed. He hummed tentatively in the shower. He watched the breakfast TV news with an involved and possessive look on his face – as if it was his world and not mine. He ate cereals with bran in them.

I still imagined I loved him. I persisted in liking the idea of him, but his actual, physical presence made me stressed and sad. He crowded me with his certainties, the way he took our happiness, his and mine, for granted. I suppose, as in the beginning, I loved him more from a distance. I loved him more when he was not there.

Then, that spring, as the evenings grew sharper and lighter and seemed to illuminate my unhappiness, as I seriously, privately, questioned the idea of spending our whole lives together – just as I was beginning, unwillingly, to face the fact that I might have made a mistake – we conceived.

By mistake, he planted a baby in me, fused our poor hearts together with a child. It wasn't his fault, but I hated him for it. I hated the potency, the deliberate energy of his sperm. Secretly, I blamed him. I blamed him in an unfair way, for relieving himself in me, blocking my only escape route with his brutal, sexual self. It seemed gross and perverse that I'd allowed him, received him. That I'd complied.

Even now, I can't understand it. My diaphragm, always so assiduously smeared with jelly, so carefully inserted and checked, must have slipped. I know there was no hole – I'd filled it with water and held it, perfectly still, over the bathroom basin for three minutes, to check. There was no rational explanation. I was simply a statistic in the small failure rate on the family planning leaflet.

'One of life's little accidents,' smiled Alistair, gathering me in his arms, ecstatic at the thought of his own capacity to impregnate. I pushed him away angrily.

And that was it, the end of freedom and choice. Accidentally, we'd made a child. Just at the point when I was seriously wondering whether I should leave him, we'd made someone who'd be a combination of the two of us – we two, who weren't a good combination at all. I was very sick. Every day I sobbed quietly to myself as I flushed my sour early morning vomit away. The doctor fiddled with a little cardboard wheel and told me with a snort of laughter that the baby was due on Christmas Day. Everywhere, doors were banging shut. Everybody congratulated us.

'Labour,' announced Alistair's mother, as she hemmed yellow curtains with clowns on for the baby's room, 'is not called labour for nothing – it's jolly hard work, believe me.' And I did believe her, because she'd had five children – all as large and keen and long limbed as Alistair – the last one famous for being born in twenty minutes as she finished cooking supper for the other four ('My helping of shepherd's pie was still warm, and I was able to finish it as I sat there on the bathroom floor, waiting for the ambulance to arrive . . .').

Only my best friend Ede guessed the truth. 'You don't want it, do you?' she said, without flinching, expertly rolling a cigarette, pinching out the tobacco and licking the paper. I looked at her, with her long white-blonde hair and her second-hand jacket. There was nothing, visually, to connect her to babies. I could not picture her in the same room as one. She had a fragile wombless quality which somehow exonerated me.

I shrugged, but could not speak. Ede knew. I didn't have to say. She knew I couldn't say it aloud, even to her, make it true – admit my life was devastated, spoiled. It was done. What was the point? How could I betray the pathetic, hopeful blob in my womb, which was at that moment enthusiastically dividing and enlarging itself? It was human. It would have clown curtains. According to my book, the heart was already beating. That morning, I had booked an abortion, only to cancel it again forty-five minutes later, the sweat setting in cold streaks on my neck.

Ede just touched my shoulder and let me look away.

It is dark when I put my key in the door – a thick and raw November dusk. I bite my lip and stand in the hall for a moment, calm and detached, like someone waiting to be asked in. In the next room, there's laughter and the sound of clapping. Alistair always leaves the radio on, for security purposes. I snap it off and go round putting on lights. I think of ringing Alistair but can't face the questioning. I think briefly of going up to paint as usual, but can hardly even face the climb up the stairs. I decide to make tea.

My sister Sara rings. 'I can't believe it, Suze,' her voice is tiny, subdued, far away, 'I've been crying all afternoon.'

I cradle the phone between chin and shoulder and sit on the sofa to take my boots off. I stare at the varnished floorboards. Alistair sanded and I varnished them when we first moved in, when we were still high on the newness of each other. I remember how we made love upstairs between coats – easy, sweaty, laughing orgasms – waiting for each layer of honey-coloured varnish to dry. I ease a squashed raisin off the floor with my fingernail.

'I know, I know,' I say without conviction, without an idea of what to say.

'I mean,' Sara continues, filling the spaces which punctuate her sobs, 'now there's no chance ... never will be. Couldn't he have called us if he was that desperate?'

'How?' I ask. 'Like he replied when I wrote to say I was pregnant, or when you were so ill ...'

Sara had been in intensive care and he knew it and made no move to contact her. I'll never forget that winter. My mother and I picking our way through the slush on the Fulham Road to reach the hospital. Sara's face, blank with pain and puffy with steroids. We didn't know what would happen. We struggled through the days, eating like tourists in pancake houses and sandwich bars – filling the gaps inside ourselves with fast food, whilst we stayed close to the hospital and waited for news. 'He doesn't like hospitals,' Penny, always his favourite, and the only one of us he still saw occasionally, had insisted, 'he was ever so sorry to hear she was ill.' We didn't know what would happen. Two and a half months later, when Sara could have been no more than dust in the air, he enquired about her at the end of a letter to Penny.

'And anyway,' I continue, 'I doubt he was desperate. He just had nothing left and that was the way he wanted it. He didn't want any of us, not even Pen, whatever she likes to think. This was just the logical next step – and it wasn't such a big step ... I expect he got himself blind drunk.' I stop. I realize I am shaking all over, my teeth chattering in my head.

'But Susan,' Sara sobs, insistent, 'to end your life ... don't tell me it was such a little thing.'

I breathe, I rock, I laugh quietly, hysterically to myself. I line my boots up on the rug so the toes kiss.

'There'll be an inquest, Mummy says. Suze? Are you there? What're you doing?'

What am I doing? I look down and notice with interest that my hands are shaking as if they were separate from my arms, puppet hands. I try to even out my breath, but it won't work. I count inwardly to ten. I won't give in. I won't give him credit for this — I won't be shocked or dismayed. I won't give him the satisfaction. But what else can I say to her? That in my heart I'm relieved he's finally gone? That the planet feels lighter, rounder, brighter?

'Oh, it's all right for you, I suppose,' says Sara, giving up, 'you've got the baby coming and you've got Alistair. I haven't got a man I can turn to. We aren't all so lucky.' As usual, I can't give her the dialogue she wants. We say goodbye and hang up. I stand very still for a moment, then go back to making tea.

As I fill the kettle, the baby, snuggled in the fluid space beneath my heart, fusses and kicks — a buzz, as the head nuzzles against my pubic bone. I shiver, and realize that something in the room feels wrong — as if the furniture has been pushed out of place. It's such a strong feeling that I look around, but everything's as it should be. I lean against the sink waiting for the kettle to boil, and turn to glance at the time on the kitchen clock. And then, just for a second or two, I see him.

He appears outlined against the fridge, swinging abruptly into focus out of nowhere, a small thin boy, turning his grey face toward me in the electrically lit gloom. His movement is blurred, exaggeratedly slow and deliberate. His eyes – empty and dead – seek the corner of the room where I stand, as if he's trying to fix upon me, penetrate my space. The sensation of his presence lasts just long enough for me to know there is appalling misery in his face.

Then, after a sharp intake of breath from me, he is gone, and there is just the fridge – white and cold and somehow oblivious.

Right from when she was tiny, Queenie loved clothes. When she was only three or four, she'd sneak off up the stairs after breakfast and they'd find her struggling into her best frock, breaking all the fastenings in her fury that she couldn't do it herself.

When she was almost five, her father sat her down and told her she'd got a little sister. She sat perfectly still, aloof and peculiar, with her perfect blonde hair, and made a point of saying nothing. He looked at her stiffly and then reached for her hand but she could feel his embarrassment, which she automatically despised, and she pulled away from him. When he finally let her go, she ran off secretly to his conservatory, where she pinched and tweaked all the buds off his best fuchsia, leaving the debris scattered brightly on the floor like blood.

Later, she emptied all her mother's jewellery into the

coal bucket and tried on all her shoes, but they didn't scold her because they said she was still their special girl. It was only when she dragged June out of her pram and dropped her on the hard hall floor that they showed their fury and her father spanked her with his slipper. She didn't care. She lay absolutely still across his knee and didn't cry. She wasn't going to let him enjoy it.

'Look, let me get this straight,' says Alistair, standing in the bedroom doorway grinning and stark naked except for his socks. 'You're telling me you saw a ghost? You actually want to call this a ghost?'

Naturally, he's laughing at me, what did I expect? Not sneering of course – Alistair's too straight and good natured to sneer. But smiling loudly – a semi-incredulous grin. As if this were just another new, entertaining aspect of the long-running joke which is Susan. He's listening to the cricket on the radio, and now he prods his tracksuit bottoms which are drying on a radiator, turns them over and puts them back.

'Al,' I reply quietly, 'I didn't say ghost.'

I didn't, actually. I said I saw a little boy and that I was very frightened. 'I know it's ridiculous,' I countered, straight after, but still I shivered as I spoke. All the same, I didn't say it, couldn't bring myself to.

'No, no,' he insists, holding up his hand, 'no, I'm enjoying this, I want the whole ghost story, tell me . . .'

'I . . .' I begin, but he silences me quickly and turns up the radio as a run is scored.

'Oh forget it,' I mutter, now, 'I'm not saying anything. I wish to God I'd never brought it up.'

It is three days later, and the first time I've tried to tell him. Most of the conversations of the past hours have of course concerned my father. That at least Alistair did take seriously.

'Sweetheart,' he said, when I told him, his face all sad and drawn, 'come here.' And then he held me close against him for a very long time – so long that by the time he released me, the ribbing of his sweater was imprinted on my cheek. Frankly, I'd now tired of the endless discussion – with mother, sisters, with Alistair. When I refused to talk any longer, and sat instead on the bedroom floor flicking through a magazine, Alistair knelt beside me and stroked my hair. 'Time to stop thinking about it now,' he said.

'I have, I have,' I replied, brushing him off, resenting the counselling tone in his voice.

'Come on,' he coaxed.

'Go away, please,' I said, as nicely as I could. He did. He went and played a game of squash with a colleague, and when he came home was visibly pleased to find me relaxing in a big hot bath.

'That's more like it,' he said, trying to be kind, and brought me a small, carefully measured glass of wine. The next twenty-four hours passed, but I couldn't help thinking of what I'd seen. Finally, I told him on impulse, to see what he'd say.

'Just forget it,' I say again, now, 'please.'

'Hey,' he says, taking off his socks, his eyes on the radio, 'no need to be like that. So I'm not even allowed to be vaguely amused at such a story?'

'It's not,' I say, tensed with an anger which surprises me.

'What?'

'It's not a bloody story, Alistair.'

'Susan' – he lays his socks carefully on the chair – 'where's your sense of humour?'

'Oh,' and I quickly lose heart, lose interest, 'it's your attitude – to every little thing I say. But if you can't see it now, I'll never make you . . . I mean, this is hopeless.'

Oh, I think, oh, so childish. These little altercations – I can't even dignify them by calling them rows – they go nowhere. I sort baby clothes into piles on the bed. Stretch-suits with poppers and tiny feet, and vests and cardigans and mittens which would fit a doll. Alistair is lost. He gazes at me.

'Darling,' he begins, standing and scratching his body all over, back and front, 'I know you're upset, I know what you're feeling . . .' No you don't. Strangely, I'm not feeling. I know that even if I want to, even if I look inside, run my fingers along the unknown ledge which is my soul, I'll find nothing. A vacant space – no bright spots and no pain.

'Can we just forget it, please?' I say again. 'I've got a terrible headache.' It's true. Small lights are dancing in the corner of my vision. I scoop the white clothes into a bundle on the bed and lie down with my arms crossed on my chest, my elbows resting on some bit of our baby. There's a ripple inside me, soft as a bubble. In the adjoining bathroom, steaming water crashes down. Alistair goes to turn off the taps.

'The human mind is very powerful,' he announces, appearing suddenly again in the doorway. 'This business has come at just about the worst time imaginable for you – I mean, with your hormones and all of that.'

Hormones. How I hate that word, that tinny, over used Alistair word – that pregnancy text-book word that explains everything about me and lets him off the hook.

'But,' he continues, oblivious, 'I think you're making too much of this, this . . . whatever it was, over-reacting. You're on edge, darling. The mind plays tricks – we all know that. Don't be hard on yourself, please, I know you.'

He wheedles, he strokes my forehead, arranges my hair on the pillow.

'When're you going to your birth class again, anyway?' he asks, thinking that's the right question, the one that will cheer me up, remind me that having babies is what I'm here for. Point me right back on course again.

I shrug and turn my head away. Then, secretly, I watch him, this man moving, naked, around the room, touching clothes, pulling at a towel, putting his watch down, with a faint, scratchy sound, on the chest of drawers. It is quite remarkable. At this moment he bears no relation to me whatsoever. I am cut off, adrift, in a separate, shadow world, where things happen in an allotted space – slow, fragmented, without proper, recognizable form. And it is form and tangibility that I crave now. Something to hang on to, to cut through the numbness. Make me feel something.

I stare at the window, the blind. I know what's out there, I don't even have to look. A bitter November night – chimneys and grey slate and TV aerials. A pinched, hopeless landscape, of walls and floors and windows – people locked into tight, meaningless, electrically lit spaces. Why, I wonder for what feels like (but cannot be) the first time, didn't my father like me? Alistair regards me calmly and strokes the base of his belly, where the wiry hair begins.

I know what he's thinking: Plan A hasn't worked.

'I'll get you some Panadol,' he says.

And that's it. That's our first conversation about it.

My father's funeral's set for Wednesday.

It's getting colder. The radiators at the clinic are not heating up properly, need to be bled. A man in overalls comes to do it. He's muscular, freckly, and sandy haired, and carries a large kid's lunchbox with Bart Simpson transfers on it.

'Bitter out there,' he remarks to Mrs Hoffman, who's reading *Harpers & Queen* on a straight-backed chair, her ankles crossed. She hesitates, nods, and adjusts her lips in my direction, sliding her handbag closer to her shins.

'I've been all over Knightsbridge this morning,' she confides, huddling her fur around her shoulders, briskly turning the page of her magazine, 'I'm pooped.'

I think of sex with Alistair, how it's dulled these days, as if a vital bit of me has gone numb. As if it's happening to someone else. I sigh, and the sigh punctures the silence dramatically, causing both Mrs Hoffman and the man to look up. 'Ah, come on,' he grins, 'can't be that bad, can it?'

Out in the hall, doors waft open and closed over thick beige carpets. The radiator hisses and spurts. The phone rings. Winter settles like an anaesthetic all around us.

1970. I squatted down behind the hen hut to pee. My long scarlet skirt sank around me. I watched a beetle on the bark of a tree. I picked at a scab on my knee. Grass prickled my bare thighs. I straightened up, stepping over the wet patch, a pool of yellow standing on the earth which was baked hard and dry from eight weeks of heat wave. A dribble of piss ran down my shin. I wiped it on my skirt.

Sara and Penny were coming across the orchard, Penny almost hidden by the long grass. Sara was wearing the favourite yellow satin underskirt and a tasselled headband with coins sewn on; Pen was draped in a pair of pink nylon curtains. We all wore brass curtain rings, hooked over our ears on strands of cotton. I leaned back against the hen hut, waiting. Inside, on the lichened wooden slats, was the head of a mallard. It was just beginning to stink.

'You'd better keep out till I've dealt with it,' I said, as we stared at it in the greenish half-light of the hut.

'Where's Daddy?' Sara asked. I tapped the duck's beak with my stick. Some black stuff dripped out.

'Somewhere, never you mind. Penny's wearing that skirt next you know.' Penny looked at each of us in turn. Sara shrugged and let it fall around her ankles.

'She can have it. I don't care. I'm going to find Daddy.'

'Well, you won't . . .' I shouted, as Sara waded into a green sea splashed with poppies and cuckoo spit, but she didn't hear me, and Penny trailed behind, forgetting the skirt. I looked around for a stone. I thought I might smash the beak, bash it flat like an eggshell. My eyes were too hot, too hard, to let me cry. If I put my eyes up to the slatted walls of the hut, I could see our father with Mrs Montoya, the teacher who lived in the bungalow next door. He was supposed to be looking after us, but he'd been in her bedroom for ages now, with no trousers on and his willy hanging out.

Penny isn't like Sara. She doesn't cry, or accuse. Instead, she says, 'I can see why he did it. I think he thought he might be ill. He mentioned some pain in a letter.'

'Some pain?' I almost shout. 'Pen, you don't kill yourself because you have a bloody headache.'

'Well,' she continues, very calm, 'what if it was something? Who'd have looked after him if he'd had cancer, for instance?'

'For God's sake, Penny, he'd have gone into hospital. He'd have had proper care, and we'd all have done all we could.'

'Would we? Come off it, Susan. I don't know about you, but I'm busy. We're frantic at the office and I've used up nearly all of my holiday already. No, it's better this way . . . it was a brave, unselfish thing he did.'

When Penny was thirteen, our mother discovered she was taking pills to tan her skin — 'A revolutionary new way to tan, from the inside, out . . .' the ad said. Mummy was furious and banned the pills immediately. 'God knows what's in them,' she said, 'they're probably poisonous — don't you care what you put into your body?'

'Not really,' Penny'd replied, her mouth hard and confident, 'I'd rather have a sun tan now. Once you're forty it's all over anyway . . .' We all laughed at her.

'He had nothing to live for,' she says now. 'You don't seem to understand, Susan. He knew what he was doing — I think he was thinking of me.'

'Penny,' I say, quietly, very carefully, 'are you not horrified?'

There's a pause, whilst she considers this.

'How do you mean?' she says.

*

'Oh, Alistair,' I say into the darkness. He does not stir. He's lying on his favourite side.

'What, love?'

'Oh, I don't know. Sometimes I worry. Do you think it's true that he had nothing to live for?' When I was about five months pregnant, I wrote my father a postcard to tell him. He never replied.

'How can I know? Don't think about this now, Suze. You're getting yourself all stirred up.' He reaches back and pats my thigh, but he's weary, I know. I do not do what I used to do and snuggle my cheek against the crook of his shoulder. A short silence.

'Oh God,' I begin again, 'how will we manage?'

'What?'

'With a child. How'll we manage? Will we be good enough parents?'

He sighs and twitches the duvet back over his feet.

'We will. What's the matter? Go to sleep, darling.'

He does, but I don't. I lie awake, imagining a telephone conversation between me and my father. It's a fantasy conversation in which he's the sort of father who rings and asks you how you've been and laughs with you about things and then says why don't we have lunch and fixes a time and place. Some little restaurant he knows, not too far from where you work. I spend quite a lot of time and concentration getting the time and place right — imagining where we might have gone had he been like that. In fact, before he rings off, the man begins to take on some of the physical characteristics of other fathers I suppose I must have known: feathery grey hairs which grow down his neck and smell of cedar wood and fresh air when you kiss him; a good, broad chest and thickening waist; a voice which cracks with laughter when you say something smart.

When I've finished, I torment myself by remembering the countless, miserable times I tried to phone him and he must have been there, but he just let it ring and ring.

two.

'Sleepwalking is common in children and seems to run in families. It peaks in adolescence but declines in the late teens. Episodes are usually triggered by anxiety.'

Then, my father's funeral. So this is it, I can't help thinking, this is what his death is like, this is how it turned out.

We get up in the dark and are on the motorway as the sky lightens to a bitter sunless yellow – as if the darkness has simply weakened and given way to something else, equally alien and unkind. On either side, ploughed fields touched with frost, crows alighting on frozen ponds. We stop at a service station for coffee and doughnuts which taste of nothing and leave a snowfall of icing sugar on the paper napkin. The day feels like his suicide – dark and small and pointless.

At ten o'clock it actually tries to snow, but by midday, when we arrive, it has turned to slush. The Crematorium waits, pink and square as a school gymnasium, flayed on all sides by an icy wind. 'God, so many cars and people,' I whisper to Alistair.

'Oh,' he says, 'there'll be several going on at once, they're in and out like nobody's business.' And he's right. Each crowd waits its turn, straining to remain separate, in the wood-panelled waiting-room. White faces, suppressed giggles, nerves. Sara already in tears, Penny oblivious, somehow at home. Our crowd – his crowd – is the smallest by far. It's a secular ceremony – the coffin just slides away. He didn't believe in God, of course.

It's very hard, looking back, to remember exactly what he did believe in. The superiority of technology, I suppose, mechanical power and the advance of science. These were the things which stirred his heart. He loved general knowledge, and made up special quizzes for us – 'Fingers on the buzzers, girls!' he'd say, and he was never so happy as when we were competing against each other in a game of his devising. He liked to watch game shows on TV.

He prided himself on his sense of humour, telling us stories of the pranks he'd played on friends during his time in the RAF. Cawthorn, for instance, whose mother had sent him a tin of Bartlett Pears, whilst on board ship for five months off the coast of Malaya.

'He just had this thing about Bartlett Pears,' Daddy told us, hardly able to contain his laughter, 'and she'd sent them all the way from Leamington Spa – they'd taken a couple of months to reach him. Every other day he mentioned they were on their way. So you can imagine his face when he discovered we'd eaten them all? "Very nice pears, Cawthorn," we said, and patted him on the back . . . I tell you, he almost cried.'

In the early days, our mother used to tell us over and

over what an 'exceptionally clever man' he was – repeating it like a mantra, as if that might make it true. As if it excused the way he hid himself away all day every day – even weekends – in his workshop, with his plans and technical drawings. He had always just invented something which he'd discover, to his chagrin, had just been patented by someone else. But when he thought he'd succeeded, his face bore a look of sublime concentration akin to love. Then we were all invisible to him. Once, he was interviewed on television about a new method of vacuum-forming in plastic, and he had that look and for a moment we didn't recognize him. Penny, still in nappies, burst into tears.

He exploded the myth of Father Christmas before I was four, and before Penny had a chance to believe at all. The Tooth Fairy, he said, was another silly fiction – he'd gladly give us more than sixpence, if we'd just throw our teeth in the bin. But it was when it came to religion that he was most scathing, and he made Sara cry one Harvest Festival when he wouldn't let her take a tin of processed peas to school for the table.

He liked crosswords and spelling. I could spell 'psychiatrist', 'diarrhoea', and 'manoeuvre' before I went to school. He read books about electronics, with diagrams of circuits chasing over the page like beetles, but never novels. He couldn't see the point in books about people.

One of his hobbies was shooting rats. Lying in bed on hot starless nights, when the sauce bottles were cleared from the Formica table, whilst our mother loaded the dishwasher and then drank her coffee alone in front of the TV, I'd hear the click of the coat cupboard in the hall and I'd know. He'd take his gun and make his way noiselessly down the drive, under a ragged moon. The light down there by the barns would be watery, the only sound his feet crunching over the shale, and the leaky tap hissing into the unmown grass in the orchard. The night air was a cloud of tiny insects waiting to be breathed in; occasionally a moth darted over the blossom in the hedge, a winged blur in the gloom.

The courtyard was surrounded on three sides by barns. This land belonged to us, but my father rented the acres and the barns to Marsden, the farmer. Every summer, Marsden's spastic son, Tommy, carried the sacks on his back and stacked them in the barns. He gave us fruit gums. Then he was discovered in a haystack with a girl and we never saw him again – 'Well, thank God for that . . .' said our mother, who could never quite bring herself to trust him. Now there was a man called Derek who was not half as nice and had tattoos of a severed heart on his forearm.

As he came close, he stopped and raised his gun, at the same time kicking the door hard. It shook on its hinges and flakes of brittle white bird shit pattered to the ground. And then it would begin. The dark bodies would slide into view – moving targets as they left one building and made a run for the next. Or else they'd pause, tantalizing him with their nearness, so that he'd hardly dare take aim in case that would be the second they'd decide to move, leaving only the swirl of a heavy tail in the dust. That was the game, that split-second decision.

He'd stay there an hour or more – for the buildings were infested – and play until his luck ran out. The sport would have an almost hypnotic effect upon him and one death would just lead to another. I knew all of this because he'd often take us up there the next morning to see the bodies, already a sticky, dancing mass of insects and entrails. This was his idea of a good time.

He had life and death all figured out. He informed us that the latter was an entirely natural phenomenon – final bodily decay, no more – not to be feared or grieved. For weren't we all just matter and particles, flung together godlessly, without wit or reason? Faith was a wicked deception, and grief pointless – a useless expense of energy. He explained this one morning over breakfast, when Sara's canary had died suddenly in the night, as he pushed a sausage around a plate which swam with egg yolk. He was so very sure of this, and he took such pleasure in telling it. A single bead of yellow clung to his lips and glistened there and his eyes shone.

Now I stare at the coffin, daring myself to seek out the space beneath the dark wood. He's more real for me now than he has been for years, because this time I know he's there, on his back, face up in stiff new Paisley pyjamas – the ones Penny sent him for his birthday a long time ago. Though they must have been in his cupboard some six or seven years, they've never been worn until now. He was always funny about new clothes, did not like them, did not like to be bought them. Something about his mother pinching him when he was a child — a ritual, a joke. So Penny gave them to the undertaker — an irony he wouldn't have enjoyed.

I realize it is some years since I pictured him whole. Head, body, and legs — a specimen suspended. I've developed a system for deleting most of him, all but the most difficult bits which will not fade. When I think of him, I see, as a rule, only a small and persistent corner of his mouth where there is a thin white string of saliva, slightly congealed, hanging there. 'Wipe it, Daddy!' we all used to chorus and delve in his pockets to pull his handkerchief out. Just as we did when he ate sausages with Colman's mustard (which he mixed with great deliberation in a wooden egg cup) and sweat clung to his hairline and dribbled down his forehead. We sometimes called him 'Gub Gub' after the pig in *Doctor Dolittle* and it's true that the Daddy of my very early childhood was a kind of animal-daddy — shambling, pathetic, but somehow harmless.

But this all changed when I turned thirteen, and I could barely suppress a shudder at his bald hands — bereft of hair since he tried unsuccessfully to put out a chip-pan fire — his fleshy face, his neck which was slightly pocked where he had removed blackheads, his thin, hairy shins.

As the coffin slides away and the kitsch little gate closes, I am shocked to feel myself relax. It's a huge comfort to know it's that body in its entirety that they are burning now, head, body, and legs, that black tail of smoke snaking up into the sky.

Later, Sara, Penny, and I stand together for the first time in his bungalow on the edge of town.

'God, it's so bare, there's nothing here,' says Sara, 'how could he live like this with nothing? Didn't he buy anything?' It's true. This is simply the cadaver of a house. No fabrics, no pictures, no clutter. No hopeful bits and pieces. We hang together, adrift, unsure where to put ourselves. Only Penny has been here before – and she just once or twice – so we can't just walk in as if we know where we are. There's nothing to connect us to the place, no one to show us around. I wonder whether he ever thought it through – ever realized that by dying he'd play host – let us all in for the first time.

'He didn't care about things,' says Penny, 'not everyone does, you know.' She walks away from us, to look out of the window. I laugh softly and the sound is odd and crazy, a shrunken thing.

'He didn't care about anything or anyone, let's face it,' I say. 'We were all too much for him. He preferred to have nothing.' Penny walks out of the room as I speak.

'She can't resist it, can she?' says Sara, blowing her nose.

'Oh, Jesus Christ,' I say, trying to jerk some pity out into the space around me, but whether for us or for him, I

don't know. I'm already in a different place from Sara and
Penny. Each is grieving in her way. They're both still
daughters. But I'm nothing, a stillborn presence – neither
existing, nor properly not existing – whose only function
is to accuse.

'Do you really need to go to the house as well?' Alistair
said, earlier. 'Isn't the funeral enough, in your state? It's
not as if you ever knew him in that house. I can't see what
you're going for. Can't you use pregnancy as an excuse?'

'Oh, I must,' I replied, 'I must support them.' But I
knew it wasn't that. I had to see.

And now that I finally stand here, it's with some relief
that I see there's nothing but the husk – dry and hard –
of a small mean man. It's just a modern bungalow, finished
with already, the house of someone who'd let go. There's
no sense of life lingering on, inhabiting the cracks and
spaces. In fact it's hard to believe he really was here until
last week – boiling the kettle, brushing his teeth, opening
cans of food, putting out the rubbish, contemplating his
death. The three of us drift apart, and I force myself to
walk into every room, looking for something I can't name,
inspecting the fixtures, the equipment, the ugly sixties
furniture. Looking for some clue.

I open the lavatory door. A roll of pale yellow toilet
paper – his toilet paper, reached for only last week – a box
of matches, three dead flies on the windowsill. I close the
door. In his bedroom, an old pair of shoes stands on a
square of maroon carpet, an offcut. In the fuzz of human
dust and fluff on the chest of drawers, a pair of unused

shoe-laces, a tin of smoker's toothpaste, a single unwrapped indigestion tablet. A valet chair I realize I remember from childhood, with a pair of pilled nylon trousers hanging on it. On the small high windowsill, a bone china ornament from Granny's house, blue tits on a branch. Above them, a perfect square of blank, white sky, no curtains. On the wall, a modern oil painting of a young woman with a short, diaphanous robe falling off one breast to expose a goose-pimpled, brown nipple. The wardrobe door is open and I jump as I catch the movement of my own reflection amongst the brown and grey clothes hanging there. Quickly, I retreat and close the door.

In the kitchen, Sara is sobbing quietly.

'He even washed up before he did it, Susan, look.' On the draining board there's one plate, one fork, one knife, a cheap petrol station tumbler with dimples and a small saucepan. 'He locked the back door, too, you know. They found the key in his pocket.' She sobs openly, her face a mess of wet mascara. I put an arm around her, but there's nothing I can say.

In the sitting-room Penny is swishing the curtains shut against the already fading light.

'We don't want people looking in,' she explains, her eyes dry, her pale face dull and unforgiving. And for one quick, awful moment I see him again.

Alistair can't be away from his office for long, so he drives back alone that afternoon. My sisters and I stay on at our mother's house for another twenty-four hours, waiting around. We all know what we're waiting for.

Mummy sits smoking endlessly discussing the reasons she left our father, sifting through the facts, repeating them to anyone who happens to be in the room. His death has brought her life sharply back into focus. She sits and stares. It isn't fair, she says, she's always done her best for everyone. She thought she'd done her best for Ray until he left her for his secretary.

'What a bloody fiasco it's all been,' she remarks again and again to Ken, who moved in six months ago. He squeezes her hand and says he'll walk the dog.

We eat cold potato salad in the kitchen, and then watch a bad film on TV so that we don't have to talk. Penny goes to bed early, before the end. Sara gives me a significant look. I sleep badly, the baby's feet giving me indigestion and making me dream that someone is standing on my solar plexus all night.

At nine the next morning, his solicitor rings and asks to speak to Penny. Outside it's rainy and dark. We wait in the kitchen in a silence broken by water falling off the roof guttering and on to dustbin lids outside, and coffee percolating. We strain to listen, but Penny – in the next room – is scarcely speaking anyway. Ken lights a cigarette. Mummy pulls a tissue from the box and tucks it up her sleeve; Sara sits very straight and tense; I wrap my hair around my little finger. Then the phone rings off and we wait for Penny to come back in, but instead she goes upstairs. Her bedroom door shuts. Without hesitating or looking at us, Mummy follows her up.

When she comes back down, she says that the gist of our father's Will is this: that Penny is the sole beneficiary of his entire estate, apart from a sum of fifteen thousand pounds which has been left to a neighbour's son.

'I didn't feel it was the right moment to ask,' says Mummy, 'but I assume she intends to share it – how could she not?' Oh God, I think.

'But she didn't say anything?' Sara asks.

'She asked me to leave her alone. She was very calm. She wasn't angry or anything, but she didn't want to talk.'

'She was expecting it,' says Sara, 'that's why.'

We all look at each other. Ken reaches out for Mummy's hand, clenched on the table. We smell the coffee burning.

I think, I hope the dead can't watch the living. I hope he doesn't have the satisfaction of seeing our faces now.

For my fourteenth birthday, I got a present in the post – a big box, light, but expensively wrapped, and it said, 'from Daddy and Granny, with love'. I tore it open. There were many layers of paper. Two minutes later, the paper lay at my feet, ripped and crumpled sheets, shiny, streaked with silver. The present? A bar of soap.

'Well, fuck them,' my mother had said gallantly, using the word on purpose to cheer me up. But I forgot I was wearing mascara for the first time, and I cried.

There's a photo of me with Granny, taken by my father, when I'm six years old, wearing a psychedelic needlecord minidress. We're standing next to her pale blue Alfa Romeo sports, which she drove around town even at the age of seventy-four, with cataracts in both eyes. Her arm is around my shoulders and I have a front tooth missing.

She was always careful with her appearance, and her tailored floral dress carefully disguises her heavy, rather shapeless bosom. Her ivory leather shoes have small expensive heels and are punched with tiny holes. Her hair was thinning by then and she wore a wig most days – if you were small you could look up and just see the black elastic which held it on, peeking through her own sparse hair underneath.

It's funny because, despite all the care about her appearance, Granny loathed cameras and, looking at the photo now, I can see it for what it is.

Even more alarming, and caught perfectly by the camera on a chill spring morning in 1967, is the expression of absolute hatred on her face. Whether of the camera, my father, me, or all three – it's impossible to tell.

Alistair meets me at St Pancras and drives me home in steady black rain, his face set in a long line of disbelief.

'It's bloody unbelievable, as if you and Sara counted for nothing. His own daughters. I can't believe you're just accepting it?'

'God, Alistair,' I reply, 'you sound as though you're blaming me. How is it you always manage to make me feel guilt for things I haven't done?' Alistair sighs the exaggeratedly patient sigh of one who is perpetually misunderstood. 'Well,' I continue, 'what else can we do? We have to wait, Sara and I. We can't force her . . . she has to tell us.' Through half-closed eyes, I watch the wet bands of blue and orange light as they wash over the windscreen, dip, dissolve and disappear. 'Anyway, it's all exactly as I expected.'

My body, only half alive over the past forty-eight hours, is waking up. I fold my hands over the warm sleeping ball of my belly and feel the backbone of my baby, stilled by the motion of the car. There's a mile of silence, swollen still with Alistair's appalled incredulity.

'I can't believe you sometimes, Susan,' he says, and he sounds infinitely hurt. 'You plod through life, half asleep. I don't know what you expect. People will always take advantage, you know.'

I swallow. I can't reply. I know this makes things worse, but still I can't reply.

'Well,' he says finally, 'it's up to you I suppose.' He fiddles with the knobs of the radio, finds Radio 3 which always depresses the hell out of me. Some plaintive orchestra against a background squeal of poor reception.

'Al,' I begin. But it's hopeless. Years of mismanagement and unkindness and guilt are impossible to explain to someone like Alistair. He's from a large, happy family. His mother loved his father, and they all got plaid dressing-gowns and jigsaw puzzles for Christmas. Is that why I married him?

Alistair gives up on the radio. I turn my face away from him and rest my cheek on the cold glass of the window, through which I see only devastation and black night.

Ede is the catalyst. She introduces us.

'Oh, Suze,' she says, a whoosh of blonde hair and cigarette smoke, stacking broken gilt chairs to make room in the tiny dumping space she calls her office, 'this is Lenny. He's from Boston, originally. Lenny, my best friend, Susan.'

She indicates a man who has just appeared noiselessly and unremarkably in the doorway. I look up from where I'm sitting on the floor. I swear I do not think anything of him then, there's no blinding flash or big attraction. He's so pale and thin that I might not have noticed him.

'Hi,' he says. He's tall and wiry like a teenager, with straggly fair hair, reminiscent, in its pallor, of cherubs and babies, but dishevelled in a somehow grown-up way. The stubble on his chin is so fair it's almost white. His eyes are tired and bloodshot and he wears a Red Sox T-shirt, crumpled and stained with deep circles of old sweat at the armpits. I feel a vague and amazed pity at the mess of him. I've become used to men who groom themselves, who wear ironed shirts and comb their hair.

'Well, you look bloody wrecked, if you don't mind my saying,' says Ede offering him a cigarette, which he refuses, with a weary extension of his fingers. 'Will you be OK for tonight?'

'Oh, God, well . . .' He shrugs, and then he gives me a long look. But I don't feel it's significant. Just an aimless gaze, as if he's so tired that he had to leave his eyes there, rather than move them on.

The gallery where Ede works is not far from the clinic, and we crammed into the corner of the Italian sandwich bar in Quebec Street in our lunch hour, drinking weak, watery cappuccinos. It was then I told her what I'd seen.

'Susan,' she said, 'my God. What does Alistair say?' There was no question, of course, that she wouldn't believe me. Ede and I met at art school, best friends from the first moment – there was proper love between us. My marriage had not really changed anything, though there was an uneasy, forced camaraderie between her and Alistair. She lit a cigarette and tried to blow the smoke away from me.

'Oh, you know Al,' I replied, and shrugged and pleated a paper napkin. (Did she? Did I?) We drifted on to other things, and laughed a bit, because what else could you say, except that from time to time Ede came back with, 'Extraordinary, really weird. My God.' As we finished our coffees we sank into a mutual silent depression, and every now and then Ede glanced my way and I could see she was worrying away at various problems connected to me.

We walked back to the gallery across the freezing Mayfair streets. I often stopped there for a few minutes on my way back to work. Today, the building was warm and brilliantly lit, ready for a private view that evening. Some pictures — a mixture of gouache and charcoal — lay framed on the floor, on cream-coloured dust sheets. A few were already hung. Boys in jeans tapped with hammers. Capital Radio played. Mugs of coffee were lined up against the skirting board on the stripped-pine floor, which bounced underfoot. Ede went to make a phone call, and I left my coat on a chair and looked around. I was about to look at the pictures they'd already hung, when I glanced down and noticed the one on the floor at my feet. It was a sketch of some ivy leaves on a wall. I tried to squat down, but the baby struggled, so I crouched instead to look more closely.

I wasn't prepared for what I saw. It was very hard to understand even at the time why it touched me, why my eyes and nose filled instantly with tears. It was only a charcoal drawing of some ivy, the leaves worked in furious black strokes. Nothing but leaves. They filled the square of paper, suffocating, a curling mass. The pointed leaves were hard, almost weighted — cracking at the tips. I drew breath and sat down, holding my belly. I didn't know what I was seeing, but I was shocked by a ferocity which I understood, as if I'd known it from before, from inside myself — something that had cut through me a long time ago and left me in some pain. For the second time that week, a premonition of total isolation washed over me. A kind of grief is the best way I can describe it.

'Hey, let's go sit in my office,' said Ede, reappearing to take care of me, 'it's much quieter.' And I rubbed my eyes and followed her, and seconds later he appeared.

'Susan's baby's due on Christmas Day, would you believe,' Ede explains to Lenny. 'Doesn't she look great?' He shrugs, and slides down the wall to sit on a pile of telephone directories, his eyes set level with mine.

'Yeah,' he says, 'she does.' I blush horribly. This is awful, I think. What's the matter with me? His gaze is intrusive to me, but I can't take my eyes away. I feel unaccountably superfluous in my pregnant state. They don't want me here, I tell myself. Sex is somehow in the air, an unmistakable force, eddying round, teasing. It occurs to me that maybe there's an excitement between them, that maybe Ede and this man are having a fling. Somehow the idea alarms me.

'I must go,' I say, struggling to my feet, with the strange and certain feeling that I'm going to miss something.

Ede comes with me to the door. It is early afternoon, but the sky's almost dark – already most of the daylight is over. A shiny white van draws up on a double yellow line to deliver cases of wine – hazard lights flashing, its exhaust pumping blue clouds into the freezing afternoon. Ede signs a chit, and gives me a hug.

'What did you think of his pictures?' she asks quietly. 'I saw you looking – they're powerful, aren't they? He's been bloody impossible to work with, of course – I'm not even sure I like him – but we're excited, he's definitely got something . . . Hey, cheer up. I'll phone you.'

Saturday, it happens again, this time in the car.

Weak, wintry sunshine dappling the dashboard. I slow

as I approach the traffic lights on the Northside of the Common and glance in my rear-view mirror. And that's it. A face – that face, grey and unmistakable, fixes me for a moment. Then the lights change.

This time I cry out, nearly swerve and crash the car. Half a shout, half a scream, as I sit trapped in a band of white morning light. Someone behind me hoots. A blush of fear burns my face and the small of my back and my armpits are soaked with sweat. Then, strongest of all, deep, heart-gripping desolation crawls over me out of nowhere.

Seconds pass, and I look again and the mirror is clear and light, and there is only the vehicle behind, but a deep and noticeable chill has come into the car. I pull off into Taybridge Road and park shakily behind a skip. Some kids run by, shouting. A man directs a lorry backwards into a side road. I think I'm going to be sick, and open the door a little way. Everything – my cheeks, my hands, the steering-wheel – is icy.

'It can't be anything,' I say to myself, over and over. But it is quite obviously something. This time, I don't tell Alistair.

1973. We watched Billy Smart's Circus on TV with Daddy.

'Look,' he said, when Gabriella Smart came on with her doves, 'just look at that little girl.'

The ringmaster said she was only eleven – like Sara. Her sequinned leotard was ice blue, and her birds were pink and mauve and tangerine. She put them through gold hoops — they fluttered but did not fly away.

'Isn't she lovely?' said Daddy, sipping his tea, and lighting a cigarette. He inhaled and glanced at me. 'Don't you wish you could do that?' Sara and Penny were rapt, but I frowned.

'How do they get them that colour? Does it hurt?'

Daddy laughed his hard, dry laugh.

'Oh, no. It's just pellets in their food — quite humane.' He breathed a tangle of smoke out through his nose. 'Goodness, she's such a pretty little girl.'

All right, all right, I thought irritably — watching her, hating her and wanting to be her, all at the same moment.

Sara is hurt and appalled to hear that our father did after all leave a suicide note, a letter to Penny.

'No mention of us, Suze, nothing, not even an explanation. You'd think we'd never been born.'

Penny calls me from her office.

'Such a lovely letter,' she says, 'and he wanted me to have the car, too.' She talks already as though he were her father, not ours. We've all agreed to tread carefully with her for the moment — give her time to tell us what she's going to do. But, 'The car?' I repeat. 'Not drive it?'

'Well, yes,' she says, with a defiant edge to her voice, 'the Mercedes. It gave him his final release — that's what the note said — so he'd like to think I'll drive it. It's worth about thirty thousand, you know . . .' She pauses, then reflects, 'Well, not that you'd get that if you resold it, I suppose . . .'

'But,' I say again, 'you mean you'd actually drive it?'

'Of course, why not?' she says, her voice unchanged, unmoved. 'It's a fabulous car. Actually, it's quite a comfort you know, sitting in it.'

On the third day in December everything freezes. I wake to four inches of snow, rooftops jagged in the blinding light. I get up, tense and excited, as if into someone else's life, leaving Alistair in bed with a sore throat.

'There's no way I'm going in feeling like this,' he says, pulling a thick frayed jersey on over his pyjamas. I watch him closely as I hook up my maternity bra. It's always oddly liberating when he's incapacitated. Something flutters in my chest. I bring him tea, a hot-water bottle, and aspirin, and leave the house just before nine.

He is standing outside under a lamppost, wearing a long grey army-style coat and, though most of his face is covered by a scarf, I recognize him immediately. His hair sticks up in white-blonde curls on top of his head like a baby's. I stand still, wondering briefly whether to run, but he's already seen me. My heart jolts. I feel intensely shy. I cannot make sense of it. There's no one else around – just the sound of a neighbour's spade scraping the path, steel singing on stone. The pavement's an unbroken blanket of white.

'Hi,' he says, staring at me so hard I feel I can't move, 'I thought you'd like a lift.' He blows into his hands. He has no gloves on. We screw up our eyes in the sunshine. The street is becalmed, struck dumb. I laugh, a pathetic, nervous, regrettable laugh.

'You don't live here,' is all I can think of to say. We stand, several feet apart, facing one another, smiling. Everything around us is white. Then he takes my arm.

'Come on,' he says, 'you're a pregnant woman and it's cold as hell and I've been waiting for you. I know where you work, I'll take you.' It's startling to hear him say so much.

'Oh, well I've got a car,' I begin to say, and I pull my arm away gently, politely. But I go all the same. Once in the car, he looks at me briefly and laughs. I feel slightly irritated, too much of a passenger.

We have to drive very slowly. There's grit on the roads. It's a day when everyone will be late. 'So how was your opening?' I ask him. He looks surprised. For the first time, I notice his face is nervous, a tiny vein shivers under his eye.

'Oh, you know,' he says, 'lots of people. Edith did a great job. You should have come.'

'I looked at your pictures,' I say.

'Ah,' he says, as if he doesn't expect this. Then, 'What about yours? Ede told me you paint. She says you're good.' Embarrassed, I take my gloves off and inspect my nails, then run my fingers through my hair to smooth it. The cold makes it crinkle up, full of static.

'Oh, well, and what do you expect from my best friend?' I say, and smile gaily, betraying the thing I care most about. I think how stupid I must sound.

'So, can I see?' he asks, without looking at me.

'Oh, no,' I say. 'No, really, you can't be serious – there's not a lot to see. I don't get much time now anyway.' A serious lie. Why, I wonder? We drive in silence, then, 'I'm sorry, but this is just so weird,' I say. 'I mean, why did you come?'

He shrugs, then grins and shakes a cigarette from a squashed packet. His hands are raw from the cold. 'Oh God, I'm sorry,' he gestures to my bump, 'I forgot.' And he puts it back again.

'It's OK.' I hug myself and look out of the window, amused.

'Well, look . . .' he begins but we both laugh. I press my fingers on my cheeks, which I know are burning. Finally, he draws up outside the clinic. He obviously does know where I work.

'Look, can I see you sometime, Susan?' he asks, suddenly abrupt and serious, as though this is what he's been building to and this is the last possible moment to ask. I'm confused. Too confused to be nice to him.

'Oh,' I begin.

'Lunch today? You have a lunch hour?'

I laugh. 'No, I don't think so . . . I mean, I do, but not today.'

'Tomorrow then?'

56

Jesus. 'No, no, I'm sorry.' I fold my arms over my vast, shouting belly. 'What is this anyway?'

And then we both laugh again, but this time without conviction, a nervous, bitter laugh, and his eyes are suddenly definite and knowing. There's nothing left to do. I walk away quickly with the sudden knowledge that there is absolutely no escape from this.

Queenie May Sanderson, twenty-nine years old, petite and blonde, with a mole on her cheek, demonstrated Singer sewing machines for a living. The mole, equidistant between her left ear and left nostril, was unique to her in her family. She thought it made her look like a film star. Little sister June, always the brightest at school, was a teacher. But Queenie earned more, had better clothes and a bit of a social life.

Mainly, she worked in large department stores around the Midlands – they always paid her fare as well as a fee – and she saw to it that she was always well turned out. Her appearance was her greatest pleasure and concern, and in fact, living at home with her parents and sister, she spent all of her earnings, after the housekeeping she paid them, to this end.

'Heavens, you're a smart girl, Queenie,' her father would say, looking her up and down in his heavy-handed, appreciative way. 'You'll be off and married before we know it.' But he said it hopefully, wishfully, and he didn't mean it, because he knew very well that Queenie sent them all packing, all of them, any young man who expressed the very slightest interest.

'What's got into her?' his wife complained. 'What's she saving herself for? Twenty-nine years old. With every year the choice narrows and she ought to know it.'

'Well' – Bert was more tolerant, soft voiced and silly whenever he spoke of his eldest daughter – 'she's a looker, she'll manage.' He crept around her when she was in the room, sneaking looks at her as she came in from work and ate her tea, passing her the sugar bowl and watching as she heaped her spoon, leaving the door on the latch for whatever time she chose to come in. His wife knew it was pathetic. It was clear that Queenie loathed him, that she loathed them all, sweeping up the narrow dark stairs in a blue haze of cologne. Well, she knew she was smart, she saw to it. She certainly didn't need Bert Sanderson – an ageing post office clerk – to tell her. She had risen above them all and would continue. She didn't care that she was almost thirty. The truth was, she hadn't yet found a man rich enough.

Her collar was delectably white and starched. She wore small amber earrings screwed to her lobes until they pinched, which made her frown a little. She scrimped to afford silk stockings. There was not a pleat, not a wave, not a blonde hair, out of place. You wouldn't have said Queenie was pretty. Her face had a petulant, downward turn, and the blonde owed itself to evenings spent locked in the bathroom with a bottle of peroxide. But she had a certain exactly judged style, and she genuinely liked sewing machines. And it was probably the former of these two qualities which George noticed when she came to Josiah Hancock Ltd. in May 1921 to give one of her demonstrations.

'Josiah Hancock Ltd. – Ladies' Knitwear and Hosiery' was painted in proud three-foot-high black letters on the factory's smoky red brickwork, as well as on the sloping tiled roof. You could make the letters out from the railway station, where the trains pulled in from Derby and Crewe and Sheffield. It was the biggest factory in town, and they had the most up-to-date equipment, including the latest Singers – hence Queenie's visit. Old Mr Josiah Hancock did not appear very often by then, so Queenie was shown into his son's office, with its oak swivel chair and leather-topped desk. The room was empty and smelled of tobacco, ink, and animal hide. A postman's clock ticked loudly on the wall.

Queenie noticed immediately that the coat on the hatstand was cashmere and wool, expensive. She wished the label were visible, and couldn't of course risk being caught looking, but she'd have given anything to know whether it came from London, and if so which store. Two heavy yellow onyx ashtrays were placed side by side on the desk, amid a heap of papers and some swatches of cloth. 'Mr. E. Hancock, Managing Director' shone out back to front in clear, tall letters on the frosted glass of the door.

After staring around open-mouthed for a minute,

Queenie arranged her lips into a pout, breathed in sharply, and seated herself on the smaller chair, pulling her skirt tight against her calves, so that their curve was faintly perceptible through the silk, and waited. The clock breathed its gentle monotone. She was just wondering whether she had time to powder her nose – and had begun to reach for her compact – when the door creaked open and a very old man put his head around.

'Morning, miss.' His eyes bulged and his head was almost completely bald except for three, maybe four, coarse, grizzled hairs – you could glimpse the letters in the glass of the door reflected in it. 'Mr Hancock won't keep you, he'll be with you in a minute.'

A second later the door opened again and you could, in retrospect, date Queenie's change of fortune from that second, that instant in 1921. It wasn't that she was consciously attracted to the blond, dishevelled young man who appeared in the doorway, but certainly something new and startling beat in her (carefully flattened) breast. Tall and slender, with light blue eyes and a slightly weak jawline, it was nevertheless – and typically – his clothes that she noticed: his waistcoat of good quality, and his necktie slightly askew. His shirt was stiff and spotless, exactly matching her own blouse, as if they had been hatched together then separated at birth.

He apologized for keeping her waiting, then offered her a cigarette. Though she loved to smoke, she refused. She could not at that moment bring herself to accept anything from him. As if already certain she would marry him, she wanted to prolong and savour this, her separateness from him. She watched him notice her legs through the skirt, and her small feet (a dainty two and a half sizes smaller than June's) strapped into their crocodile-skin shoes.

He gazed and she gazed back.

Queenie did not know, then, what sex was. But she understood very well effective visual display. Some keen sewing machine operator's shark instinct in her recognized that here was a chance, a possibility of power. She was embarrassed to feel sweat gather on her upper lip.

She didn't know what or why it was, but at that moment when her eyes met his, she knew she was halfway to some-where – that she'd been invited, and would go. She squeezed her thighs together, relishing the texture and flop of her expensive camiknickers, and narrowly resisted the impulse to shriek aloud with a dark anticipatory delight.

The encounter with Lenny hangs around me all day like an extra layer of happiness. 'You're very chipper today, Susan,' remarks Mr Sudbury as he comes up the back stairs after a smoke.

'Ah, well,' I say, as I hand him the next patient's notes, 'you're supposed to enter a calm and serene phase at the end – it's the hormones.'

All the regular patients in the waiting-room look at me possessively. I am their child, their pregnant child.

'Goodness, hormones,' shudders Mrs Rees, nursing a stiff shoulder, 'thank God that's all over for me!'

'You have a real bloom, Susan,' Mrs Hoffman remarks, ignoring Mrs Rees as she invariably does. 'You're one of the lucky ones. I was sick every day with both of mine — every day, I tell you, I lost so much weight I was mere skin and bones.'

And it's true, I am blooming — a flower opening out; bright and soft and noticed.

At home, Alistair potters around all evening in his dressing-gown, and I grill some lamb chops, which we eat in front of the TV. A lurking guilt, coupled with a dragging exhaustion, stops me going up to paint. We watch an alternative comedy show, but I can't laugh and instead I sink into a daydream in which I'm wandering the icy streets with a tall figure in a grey coat. In the dream, I'm not pregnant any more, but lithe and heartless, clothed in inky blue, my hair tied back with a piece of string, and I sneak my fingers into his deep rough pocket to warm them.

I clear up the supper things and, as I go to put the empty milk bottles out on the door step, catch my reflection in the hall mirror, and am startled by the excitement on my face. As I clean my teeth, I feel the baby suddenly insatiably active, twitching and stretching its limbs inside me, as though my own mood were infectious. I sit down on the closed lavatory seat and hold half my body in my arms, amazed.

sleepwalking

In bed, Alistair sighs and blows his nose and runs his hands over the blue-veined insides of my thighs. I turn and kiss him, but cannot be bothered to let our mouths intermingle all that much, and soon heave over on to my side and caress his prick so he can enter me without squashing the baby. We are cupped together like measuring spoons. He whispers in my ear and spills into me, but I think I am asleep before he's finished.

When I awake with a jump, a few hours later, I know that he has been standing there for some time.

The bedroom door is half open between us, but he's been staring at me through it for several minutes. My scalp and neck grow hot with the realization that I'm awake. Oh, God. His face is white like a sick person's face, and his eyes are lit with live anger. His face is both young and much older – miserable, vicious and unloved. He is naked except for a dirty pilled vest and long knickers and this time I see clearly that his left leg is encased in a heavy metal calliper.

I lie frozen, my limbs moulded to the bed, to each other. My lungs let my breath out in a series of painful shudders. In his sleep, Alistair smacks his lips and turns away from me. This time, the boy does not take his eyes from my face.

Whole seconds pass. All I can think is: My God, my God . . . it's happening again. My head is full of blood, of fear. Then I sense something relaxing in the room – a click, a white release – and I know he's going and, keeping his head straight and stiff, he turns slowly through a complete axis, like a sleepwalker. The calliper drags on the floor, shaking his small leg, but makes no noise. Somewhere between the third and fourth step he's really gone, the landscape of our room – chairs and shoes and clothes – reclaiming the space he filled. The breath in my mouth is jagged with fear.

Alistair finds me on hands and knees on the floor among the dressing-gowns and magazines. 'Hey, darling . . .' he says and pulls me back to bed, stroking my head, but he's asleep again almost instantly and I am left staring into the night, stricken by a sudden pregnant urge to pee.

There's no way, though, that I'll leave the bed and walk through that door.

Remembering to turn down the heat under the mulliga-tawny soup, Queenie poured her son a Scotch and mixed a sweet Dubonnet and lemonade for herself – something she always looked forward to before lunch. It was a bleary Saturday in October, 1974. Wind rattled the bamboo sticks in the porch.

Blowing his nose, Douglas sat heavily down on the grey wool sofa, and lit a cigarette. Queenie watched as he wiped at the insides of his nostrils with his handkerchief. She could not stop a small, self-congratulatory smirk from crossing her face as she shook some cocktail biscuits on to a plate and adjusted a stray Kirby grip in her hair.

'Can I have an ashtray, Mother?' he asked, without looking up, holding the mounting tail of ash on his cigarette upright, flicking through a manual, something to do with his work.

Queenie relaxed and allowed herself to smile properly. Saturday lunchtimes really were the highpoint of her week now since Barbara was no longer around and she had him all to herself again. Like the good old days when he still lived at home with her, her bachelor boy, home from National Service. She'd really loathed him as a child but, once he grew up and towered over her, she noticed him for the first time. It was a funny thing but, once the quiet, sulky boy had turned into a man (a man, it had to be said, who took no notice of her, even brushing her off at every opportunity), she found the tables were turned and it was she who craved his attention.

The turning point came when he was about fifteen, some ten years after George's death. It was a Sunday morning, and she sat in bed in her quilted jacket, with tea and toast, varnishing her nails. She'd had both pots balanced on the tray on her leg, the varnish and the marmalade. Douglas had appeared suddenly in the doorway in his dressing-gown, his face creased with hatred. She'd waited, her nails spread, her face surprised, to see what would happen next. He spat a word out, under his breath, then moved away, out of the doorway, across the landing to the bathroom. She couldn't be sure, but she thought the word was 'bitch'.

After that, she craved his company and attention, couldn't get enough of him, and he retreated back to what she supposed was a plateau of behaviour acceptable to them both. Her tall, unsmiling son, on the verge of manhood — a perfect escort for this new phase of her life. Occasionally they went to the cinema together, and she hung proudly on his arm. When he went into the air force for his National Service, she felt properly widowed for the first time. She had to take tranquillizers for six months.

'He stayed with me until he was thirty-two,' she told her neighbour, Mrs Foxley, who did not have children, just a poodle called Louis who wore a yellow rhinestone collar. 'I think I spoiled him for marriage — no wife was ever going to match up, and particularly not that Barbara. Still, he's had the experience now; learnt the hard way, I suppose.'

They'd had such nice holidays in Torquay together later, mooching up and down the promenade, listening to the brass bands, smoking and drinking cocktails in the bar — perfect evenings spent watching TV in hotel bedrooms together.

And now, even though he lived a mile away, in the next village, it was back to how it should have been, just the two of them. And he always knew the spare room was there, if he wanted it. Her bungalow was in Limetree Close, a quiet new estate with small, shrubby gardens. She'd had hers crazy-paved over the first week she moved in — she found the tangle of greenery glimpsed through her violet slub silk curtains infinitely depressing and preferred the neat, flat expanse of stone. Apart from the Foxleys, who'd step over the low fence at all hours with little offerings of fruit pie or cake on a paper doily — which, not liking

desserts, she binned as soon as the door closed behind them
– she hadn't bothered with anyone in the neighbourhood.
But she watched from behind her curtains as they washed
their cars, did their paper rounds, or went into Burton
Joyce to get their hair permed on Saturday mornings.

'So, Douglas,' she said, now, as she crossed the room with
the purple glass ashtray, her nylon skirt-lining swishing
pleasingly against her stocking tops, 'what did you think
of the Eurovision Song Contest?'

The very next day, when the snow is compacted hard and
turning to ice, he calls in at the clinic. It's almost
lunchtime.

Hot with surprise, I lead him into the waiting-room and
he stretches himself on a burgundy velvet chair whilst I
self-consciously make a couple of phone calls. He doesn't
look right at all – long and vivid and out of place. He
folds his arms and gazes at the pictures on the walls –
deadpan cows and horses on careful grassy landscapes –
each one lit by its own private spotlight, a neat brass tube
shooting out a prim fan of light. The osteopaths all glance
at Lenny as they come in and out; I suppose heavily pregnant women do not usually have boyfriends.

'Well . . .?' I say, when I've finished the calls.

'Will you come out for a bit?' he asks, frowning a little,
as though he expects me to say no.

First we walk, briskly, hardly talking, because it is so

cold. The air stings my cheeks, chafes my ankles, prickles the skin of my belly through my clothes, where it's stretched tight over the limbs and back of my child. I think, with a sudden and pathetic pang of longing, of the clingfilmed tomato sandwich waiting in my desk drawer, and wonder what on earth I'm doing here with this man. Then we sit on a bench in the middle of Berkeley Square, where grass pokes up through the thawing snow, and watch a small dog pissing meticulously on each separate blade. After some uncomfortable silence, he tells me that I'm beautiful.

'I haven't been able to stop thinking about you, since the other day. You must have known.'

I cannot help it. I laugh. Me, in my plum-coloured maternity dress and support tights, the lapels of my outsize coat hardly meeting in front. Made hot and sweaty by the extra heartbeat inside me, pink cheeked even in the frost. What a joke. Then I blush.

'Well, you pick your women well, I must say,' and I instantly regret the sarcasm in my voice. 'I mean, very married, almost nine months pregnant – what can you think of me?'

With admirable daring, he places one long gloved finger on mine. Frayed black wool, ragged so I can see the pale half-moon of his nail through it. The touch – so unexpected and deliberate – causes something to tighten in my chest and throat.

'Are you very married?' His finger scorches into mine. I

wonder whether I should take it away. But I leave it there, and I'm silent for too long a moment, before I answer.

'Yes, of course I am.'

He considers this. Does he believe me? Do I want him to? For a moment, a risk hangs there, and we both ignore it. He takes his hand away and hugs himself and looks around the square. He breathes out, a long breath, a smoke signal in the frozen air. I take pity on him.

'Well, really,' I add, more gently, and then grind to a halt. He smiles but says nothing. I bite my lip, suddenly sick of these significant pauses, intimating a situation where none exists. He's playing with me. 'Well, I'm sorry,' I say, 'but this is silly. I mean, why don't you go out with Ede? I really don't know what we're doing here.'

For the first time, maybe, I dare to look straight in his face. Clever grey eyes. We look steadily at one another and my stomach dives. We don't flirt. We've moved beyond that.

'This is a subtle thing,' he says, looking away from me now, leaning back and looking at the sky, 'I do want you, but I'm not just looking for an affair, not in the way you think. I know you're married.' I'm about to laugh again, but stop myself in time as I notice his trembling cheek and the effort this much is obviously costing him.

'Look, I'm touched . . .' I begin.

'This is a subtle thing,' he says again. 'It's not the way you think. I wanted to tell you what I felt, that's all.' Oh, I think, that's so American! The elevation of sex to something mystical – who does he think he's fooling?

'I don't know what "thing" you're talking about,' I say to him. 'I only just met you. I mean, I'm flattered, but you're just a friend of Ede's as far as I'm concerned.'

He shrugs and laughs and looks away and we get no further than that. The dog is urinating again on the frozen lawn. We decide we are cold beyond belief, and go to an Italian bar and drink cappuccino. His remarks have killed all possible conversation, so we listen to those around us, so quiet and solemn that we must look like lovers.

On the way back to the clinic, he tells me he was born in Singapore, to American parents, and had two older sisters. Both his parents were architects. One day, when Lenny was seven, his father was stung by an insect in the garden and died, right there on the grass in front of him. It was all very quick. One moment he was throwing a baseball and the next he was face down in the turf. He was thirty-one years old.

The family returned to Boston for good shortly after that, and Lenny first stepped off the boat on to American soil with his father's remains clasped in his arms, because neither his mother nor his sisters could bear to touch the urn.

That night, I dream I am in labour. Even in my dream I know it cannot be the real thing, because four smiling midwives – two at each hand – are manicuring my nails bright wound red.

'Blood colours are just right for babies,' they say, in chorus, and they tell me they will stitch up my hole with crimson thread once the baby is out. I realize without surprise that one of the midwives is Penny.

'Daddy isn't too keen on babies,' she says as she draws the brush down the centre of my thumbnail, 'you know that. How could you do this to him, Susan?'

I wake (I always do) just as the baby's head is about to emerge, to find Alistair standing over me with a cup of tea. His shoulders are still specked with water from his shower, and a scarlet towel is tucked around his waist.

'I think you were dreaming,' he says, looking perplexed and rather young — there's a new, unsuccessfully squeezed pimple next to his nose — and not at all like a man on the brink of having a family.

I was always a nervy child. But after my mother left my father and the court decreed that we had to visit him every other weekend, it got so bad I used to jump when the toaster popped up.

The biggest worry, at the time, was that he might vent his anger violently — on himself or us. I remember my mother on the phone to the police, two days after our escape. 'Yes,' she said, frowning and stubbing a gold-tipped cigarette out in an overflowing ashtray on top of the telephone directory, 'yes, he has an air-rifle of some sort.' Fingers of fear jabbed at my brain.

I was glad that she'd left him. For four years, we'd witnessed their unhappiness. Standing in pyjamas at the open playroom door, I'd seen him take a silent breath and knock her to the floor, breaking the Perspex door of my Sindy house and scattering Play-Doh and crayons everywhere. Then he smacked her again and again – hard, heavy smacks which rang out like laughter, and seconds later we watched as he smashed his car into Penny's crocus pots, leaving a heap of glistening plant flesh and soil, before tearing off into the black March dusk.

It was not surprising that she had another man. She fell in love with Ray – tall and vain, with a film-star groove in his chin – in the snack bar at the Leisure Centre where, together, they took us all swimming every Sunday morning. In that steamed-up glass room over the pool, redolent of Max-pax coffee and chlorine, whilst we all hung over the rail, wet hair stuffed into our anorak hoods, they held hands under the Formica.

She was young and pretty then, with waist-length auburn hair, which crackled when she brushed it out. She set it in Carmen rollers, and collected us from school wearing blue suede hotpants with a butterfly embroidered on the bum pocket. She said 'bloody hell' and 'damnation', and had thirteen pairs of shoes – suede and patent, as well as raffia sandals with flowers on. She wore sunglasses, pushed up on top of her head, even in the rain.

'My mother says your mother thinks a lot of herself,' said Henrietta Jarvis at school. But Mummy just laughed:

'Well, tell her that her mother's right — if you don't think a lot of yourself, no one else will!'

I adored her strength and her gaiety. She was right about everything and braver than I could ever be. I grew into a shy, unremarkable teenager, lurking in the shadow of her vivacity.

My father always said he'd never let her go or, if she ever did, then it would be with nothing. 'You came with just a suitcase,' he said, 'and that's how you'll go.' So when she left so secretly and successfully in the middle of the night — with all three of us, all our pets and half the furniture — he could not forgive her. Or us. In fact, he spent the rest of his life devising suitable punishments.

This was 1972. Our ages at the time were twelve, ten and eight.

On a Saturday night during one of our weekend visits, he sat us down and quizzed us about Ray.

'Well, does she sleep with him, then? Does he spend the night? You three should know — you live in that house of sin . . .' We said we didn't think so. It was true that Ray came round a lot. We saw Mummy kissing him once — proper kisses with mouths mashing together — and he did once or twice stay on a camp bed up in the playroom, but we didn't mention this.

'All right,' said Daddy, 'I've reached a decision. I've decided that tonight you three can go back and sleep at your mother's house, since you're all so happy there. She can be the one who's inconvenienced, for a change. We'll see how she likes it. Ah, but . . .' and he held up a finger, 'perhaps we'd better telephone first to see if she's there?'

He dialled. The phone clicked and whirred. We sat in a dejected row on the sofa, waiting. Then he replaced the receiver.

'No answer.' He was cool, grim, determined. A little vein throbbed in his temple. 'I'll try again in a few minutes, shall I? I'm sure if she cares at all about you, she won't be out for long. Meanwhile, you can get your things together . . .'

Upstairs, in silence, we packed our zip-up holdalls. We packed up the golden hamster, Tin-Tin, who always travelled with us. Brown paper bags of sunflower seeds were lined up on the hall shelf. Again and again, Daddy dialled the number. Penny turned suddenly to Sara and me and said brightly, 'We love our Daddy, don't we, girls?' Her tone was hopeful, hurting, frantic. Sara made a sound, half sob, half laugh, but I said nothing. And we sat on in a row, our knees six sharp grazed points of flesh.

'Well,' he said, finally, at a quarter to eleven, long after we should all have been in bed, 'still no reply. I think we'd better assume she's out with him, hadn't we?' He snorted, triumphant. 'You see how much she cares about you — I bet she can't wait to be shot of you on a Saturday night. I've a good mind to dump you on her doorstep, but I suppose if she's out having sex somewhere, she might be all night. So you'd better unpack and stay here after all.'

As usual, he was vindicated. And we tramped upstairs again – miserable, exhausted, chastened.

Alistair says he'll take me out to eat.

'It's been ages,' he says, ruffling my hair, 'and once the baby's here that'll be it . . .'

We go to a restaurant with sawdust on the floor and sour-faced waiters with jet studs in their ears. Alistair wears a tie and seems madly, ridiculously happy. He smiles at me and scans the wine list as if he'd written it himself.

'Hey,' he says, 'maybe we should have champagne.'

'Champagne?' I echo, tired and far away. He gives me a long look.

'Well, and why not?' He gazes straight at me for another moment. I pick a dark crystal of sugar up on the end of my finger. 'Celebrating the end of our freedom and so on. Don't play with the sugar, Suze.'

I let the crystal melt on my tongue, and shrug and try to smile and look excited because, after all, I've done nothing wrong. There's no reason why we shouldn't still all have a happy life together – Alistair and this baby and me. I take his hand across the table and squeeze. The flesh is hot and solid, with a layer of fine hairs, and I examine it, surprised, wondering at its separateness from me. I am struck by the thought that one day this hand will be dead – we'll all be dead, even our child. It's a fact. Regardless of what we do now, we'll still all die in our different, awful ways.

He squeezes my hand back.

'What're you thinking, sweetheart?'

'Oh, you know,' I say, 'the usual things – babies, make up, dry-cleaning . . .'

three

'Sleepwalkers are unresponsive to their environment.'

We coast, we drift, Alistair and I, towards the birth of our child. We're two irrevocably separate vessels, pulled along on the same slow current. We bob, dip, surface, spring apart, and ride together again. The distance between us comes and goes. Sometimes we're still obliviously tender with one another – pretending this is normal and that what's gone before was someone's mistake, someone's bad mood – and there's a grim comfort in this. But mostly we're remote, hopeless.

So I spend every lunch hour that week with Lenny – in sandwich bars and on park benches. It turns out that he is right – it is a subtle thing, as he said. There are no rules, no judgements to be made, no demands. He is quiet, clever, insistent. He reaches out to me, and leaves me no choice. I realize with surprise how lonely I've been.

There's nothing between us. I hardly know him. His exhibition gets a review in a national newspaper. They call his pictures 'dark and unsettling' – he says nothing, but I can tell he is extremely pleased. Twelve of them sell almost instantly, and he gets a commission. For four days we just sit and talk, as if nothing were real and yesterday and tomorrow were some poor fool's joke.

I am amazed by him. He has the head of an angel, with his white baby curls, and the body of a teenager – long limbed and sleepy, no male rough edges, no ego, no hidden agenda. But there's also something grown-up, a dark energy, impossible to ignore, which draws me in, negating the possibility of a struggle. We hardly touch, we haven't kissed. But on the third afternoon he takes off my gloves and strokes my fingers again – each one separately, so slowly I want to cry out. Another day he puts an arm around me and touches the softening which used to be my waist, where my child stirs, upside-down. But it's more than I can bear and I push him back, weakened, ashamed. 'No, I can't, please . . . you know I can't.'

On the edge of the grass verge, a man shovels chestnuts in molten coals, the wad of white paper bags flapping a surrender in the bitter wind. He smiles and winks at us – a kindly wink because we are so very obviously a couple.

I tell Ede, on the phone. I try to convey it casually, watered down, as if I'd meant to tell her before, but she knows me too well. She lets out a long breath. 'You're sleeping with him?'

'No!' I am appalled. 'No, of course not, it's not like that, we just talk. I'm about to have a baby for God's sake, Ede . . .' It's a subtle thing.

But I'm protesting to myself of course, not her.

Suicide is a death which leaves its traces – a metallic echo in the mouth, like blood.

I try to explain my father to Lenny, but find myself stuck, short of words. It would be good if he'd gone the same way as Lenny's, I think – if an insect had bitten him, if he'd just toppled to the ground before he had a chance to be bad.

'I've been seeing something,' I tell Lenny quite suddenly one day, surprising even myself as we gaze into a shop window on South Audley Street. There's a stuffed animal's head mounted on a plaque, its teeth bared, its mouth black, its tongue artificially red, like lipstick.

'Something?' He looks at me. He's not surprised. This lack of surprise somehow renders me safe.

'This boy, a little child . . . three times now.'

He looks at me again, waiting. He doesn't laugh. I think he knows what I'm going to say next. But I say it anyway, 'I'm scared. I'm scared of it.' I'm stuck, I think. I'm stuck inside a strange gelatinous substance which is the future and it has set – cold and dark and hard – before I've had a chance to move.

It becomes clear that Penny does not intend to share any of the money. She never says it in so many words, but the fact is simply there one day, unavoidable and large. She hasn't phoned any of us over the past ten days and it's hard to catch her except at work.

'Give her time,' says our mother, her voice all sad and brittle, 'she's grieving still. She loved him, you know, in her way . . .'

I'm about to protest, but I stop myself. I say nothing.

Alistair does not come up to the loft very often. He can't understand my painting. But now his head appears through the gap in the floor which opens down to something between a staircase and a ladder.

'A cup of coffee,' he says, brightly. 'I suppose we'll have to childproof all of this, won't we, eventually?' He looks around as he puts the mug on the floor, and his eyes rest on my canvas. 'Good Lord,' he says, 'who's that? What a miserable little chap — looks like one of those Victorian paintings by, oh, you know . . .'

'Do you like it?' I hear myself asking, suddenly mesmerized by the stripes on his shirt, all so navy, all so straight. He gives me a tender look.

'Well, I don't know,' he says, ever honest, 'I mean, it's a bit grey, isn't it?'

I go for my check at the hospital, my second appointment with a consultant. I ask Alistair whether he wants to come too, but he has client presentations all day.

sleepwalking

'Do you think you'll need me?' he asks, stuffing his squash kit into a bag. He does not look at my face, so he only hears the answer, which is negative.

The hospital is busy, the midwives rushed and unsmiling. Women in all stages of pregnancy wait, legs splayed, bored, mostly alone, in a great room with information about HIV and dental care on the walls. There's an empty plastic water-dispenser with a mountain of discarded paper cups below, and a pile of weaning charts on each pale yellow Formica table. I am put in a room and asked to undress down to my underwear and lie down. I wait, alone, for ten minutes listening to feet in the corridor, then a man comes in, apologizes for keeping me waiting, covers my torso with a piece of paper towel, and leaves again. The towel sits ridiculously on the curve of my belly and finally wafts to the floor in the draught from under the door. I sit up and wait, shivering.

Finally, the consultant appears, three identical dark-haired students trailing behind him. He nods towards my head, asks me to lie down, and places an icy hand on me.

'Measure the height of the fundus, please,' he says to one of the students, and a tape measure is laid along the most extreme point of the curve. I shudder.

'No,' the consultant's breath smells of coffee and cigarettes, 'feel first with your hands – how can you know where it ends?' He takes the student's hand and prods hard just under my ribs. It hurts. A small kick replies from inside. The beginnings of tears sting my nose. 'Now, assess the age of the fundus.' The consultant scans the students' faces,

'You . . .' He motions to the one who hangs back, the one who looks the most afraid of being picked. Sadist, I think, with a surprising amount of venom. Reluctantly, the student begins to press his hands on my stomach, putting an unbearable pressure on my bladder.

Suddenly I know. I see the door, still ajar, the slice of empty corridor. 'Excuse me,' I snap my legs shut, knocking a box of tissues to the floor. I grab my long sweater from the chair and stuff my head through the hole, the static of my hair crackling loudly.

'Now then, Mrs . . .' The consultant looks for my name.

'Here,' I dump the phial of urine, warmed by my fingers, into his hand, and I'm down the corridor before they can stop me, by a stroke of luck still wearing knickers, by another choosing the right direction. I jab at the lift button with my finger and as the door finally opens I collide with Lenny as he tries to step out.

'I came to wait for you,' he says, staring at me because I have no skirt on, only my sweater flapping round my thighs.

And then I'm crying, and I step – one small, easy step – towards him and put my fingers on his neck, and press myself and my child against his safe, quiet form.

Heavily, Daddy sat down on his valet chair to put his shoes on, using a shoe horn made of hard yellowing bone. I sat on the bed, on the dark red satin eiderdown (under which I was apparently conceived one forgettable October night), and held a hot-water bottle against my head. I had my first earache. I was four years old.

My eyes were still shining, my lashes wet, from the tears of half an hour ago. I could see myself reflected in the gleaming wood of the wardrobe next to the bed. In my ear, the roll of water on rubber. My daddy was tying his shoe-laces, oblivious. He whistled under his breath. I frowned, trying to think of something to say, something which would bring him back, make him see me.

'Show me the lady picture, Daddy, please.'

That was it. He glanced at me and reached up, smiling, up on top of the wardrobe for the picture, torn from a magazine. The lady had long black princess hair, and black eyebrows and lashes. She was sitting astride a chair, as if it were a horse, and she had no clothes on at all. Just bare lady's nipples. 'And what's her name?' I knew the answer because I'd asked it before. He took a long look and calmly replaced the picture up in the dust on the wardrobe.

'Christine Keeler,' he said, almost to himself, 'she's a model girl. My pin-up.' He fiddled with his cufflinks. 'Don't tell Mummy.'

Lenny takes me straight to his place. A rule is being broken and we both know it. He doesn't have his car, so we take a taxi. He wraps his big coat around me. We do not speak. We watch the December streets move past us. Tears evaporate on my cheeks, drying in the artificial, air-freshened warmth of the cab.

The street where we stop is lined with office stationery shops and sandwich bars. Only a scattering of TV aerials give a clue that people live here. We go up steps next to a dry cleaner's, big glass windows and green and yellow signs. A man nods to Lenny from inside, evidently noticing me. I wonder what he can think.

Inside, the hall is freezing and dark, the stairs steep, uneven and dirty. There's a smell of cat's piss, of uncollected garbage; there's a bicycle propped against the wall. I perk up a little. It's a long time since I've been to a strange, dirty place.

'It's a mess,' says Lenny, as we step inside his flat at the top of the second flight, 'I don't generally have people round.'

He clears a space on the sofa for me, chucking newspapers, blocks of sketching paper, and paint catalogues on to the floor. The wastepaper basket by the sofa overflows with orange peel, and the oily smell fractures the air. I snuggle back against the cushions, his big coat still around me. The room is very bare, almost empty of furniture. There's only the sofa, some floor cushions, and a long table stacked with books (as well as a pudding basin full of shrivelled conkers, and a honey container in the shape of a bear). There are some rolls of canvas leaning against the wall, some wooden frames without canvases. There's a leather jacket hanging on the door that I've never seen him wear.

sleepwalking

He lights the gas fire, and turns on lights – it's practically dark outside even though it's barely two o'clock. I watch the rows of pale blue flames turn to violet, then orange. I hear him filling a kettle in the next room. 'I'm making you tea,' I hear him say, 'then you're going to sleep.' Oh, I think, with a small, childish disappointment. He comes back in, pulls off his boots, squats down on his haunches in front of the fire, looks at me and laughs.

'What?' I smile. His happiness is bright and large and delicious. He looks different, thin. It occurs to me that I've almost never seen him without his coat on.

'Having you here . . . it's weird. You look kind of weird amongst my things.' He gazes at me, then laughs again and stretches the palms of his hands out to the flame.

'Oh, thanks,' I mock. But I know in that moment that I would do anything for him.

He brings tea and we drink it in front of the fire – ten perfect rows of red heat.

We glance at each other. The room is quiet, only the hiss of gas. We've never been alone like this. His coat slips from my shoulders. I wait and wonder. I am so still I can feel the baby's heartbeat pounding, double time, on top of my own.

In his bedroom, we sit close together on the edge of the bed and, carefully, as if I were a bubble that might burst, he puts his arms around me, and I smell the warmth of his scalp, his skin, his sweat. He slides a warm hand down my hair, to my neck, inside my sweater to the edge of my shoulder blade, where it hesitates, and I freeze. This is the moment that can't go forward or back.

He says nothing. He releases me and lifts my impossibly spherical body between the sheets, pulling the blanket up over my shoulder and smoothing my hair behind my ears.

'Sleep,' he whispers, and lets his hand rest on me for a moment and I fall straight into a dream where tiny grey birds, the size of moths, are flying at fantastic speed straight into my face.

When I wake the room's dark except for the blue dark of the gas fire, and the street lamp spilling through the patched blind. Lenny's lying on the bed next to me, awake and watching, wearing the Red Sox T-shirt he had on when I met him, and jeans. Bare feet. The digital clock says five fifteen. I know I have to go. But before I can move from the bed, he puts a hand on my thigh.

'Susan . . .'

I'm hypnotized by the light pressure of his fingers, the warmth from his wrist.

'I have to pee,' I say, struggling to my feet. I have the tiny, constricted bladder of late pregnancy, every organ pushed to one side to make room for the baby. I return from the bathroom and stand, looking for my shoes.

'I love you,' he says, regarding me steadily.

'What?' I whisper, disbelieving.

'Come here.' He says it gently, quietly, but doesn't wait

for me to reply. He gets up and takes both my hands and brings me back to bed, making my limbs move this way and that, kissing my ears, my hair, my wrists, and I feel an ache of desire ricochet inside me – a secret pulse springing back into rhythm.

'I can't do this,' I say, without conviction.

'I do, I love you,' he whispers and, as I sob one ragged sob, 'We won't do anything, I promise. I just want to look at you,' and he moves his mouth on to mine. I find tears are streaming down the sides of my cheeks, into my hair, tickling the tops of my ears.

'I'm sorry,' I say, so quietly only the baby will hear, in fact not with my lips at all because they're all used up with his kiss. He pauses a moment, looks at my face, and sweeps his whole hands across my cheeks, through my tears, then – without any more hesitation and despite his promise – peels my clothes from my body, turns me this way and that on the bed until I cling to him fiercely, pull his hard, clothed body to mine.

And it's as if he's practised. He already knows what to do with a pregnant woman. He turns me on my back and quickly unzips his jeans and kneels between my legs, still clothed, close, yet keeping his weight off me, watching my face all the time as he moves around inside me. And when I come all the shadows in the room combine and turn to light and my face is hotter than the gas fire, hotter than all the gas fires in the world put together.

'Darling,' he says, and rocks back on his heels and kisses

both my kneecaps. I struggle and pant. I have to sit up, on all fours. The orgasm has contracted my belly so it hurts.

'In a little while,' he says, stroking the arch of my spine as I rock the weight of the baby and disperse the contraction, 'we should do it again. Slowly.'

1922. Queenie and George's wedding night was not a success. Not that this, a small enough thing in itself, should (or would) have mattered – but the unfortunate fact was that Queenie held that night against him for the rest of his life.

She allowed it to seep through and infuriate her, tainting everything like a bad smell. It spoiled absolutely any pleasure she might have found in their relationship. That was it as far as she was concerned. Never again discussed or referred to by either of them, the fact remained all the same, hard and cold, a stone embedded in her gut. She could not forget. She had no natural pity.

The reception had been a grand and expensive affair. A champagne dinner at the Black Boy Hotel in Stoney Street, with its depressed grey view over the canal and the railway station. It nearly bankrupted her poor father.

'Don't imagine we'll be able to do this for June, too,' he remarked in complaining tones to his wife, as he paid the last bill. Grand it was, all the same, for Albert Sanderson to see his eldest daughter married off to the son of the town's most prosperous manufacturer. Grand, too, for her mother, Violet, to see that Queenie had – finally – caught such a nice straight tall young man. Well, she'd said he was the one, right from the start.

'Very glad to meet you, Mrs Sanderson,' he'd said, smiling, that summer's night as he stood in the hall in his car coat, waiting for Queenie to come down. He was tall and fair with a good voice – not posh, but clear as a bell – and full of confidence. Queenie said he'd not gone to the war on account of having hammer toes or some such, but you'd never have known it to look at him – he looked like he knew a thing or two. And he hadn't rushed away, either, but had been pleased to drink a glass of sherry with them in the front room, whilst Queenie impatiently rattled her door keys. Ever such a nice young man, he'd even complimented her on her collection of paperweights.

'He's the one,' she'd told Bert, that night. And hadn't she been right? The first wedding in the family this century. And Queenie, of course, looked a picture in her ivory lace dress, with the short veil and pale yellow roses. Never inclining her head or moving towards them, she greeted and spoke to people as if in her sleep, the space between her lips hardly showing. She never blinked, her eyes betrayed nothing. She seemed at one and the same time unbroken, unbreakable, yet not quite whole. Queenie could be happy without smiling.

All that money . . . June couldn't help thinking, as she picked hungrily at the roast meat. And it was what everyone else was thinking too, as they moved carefully around one another in that candlelit autumn room. The happy couple were leaving for Paris in the morning.

In the bedroom, George had champagne on ice. To Queenie's relief, he emerged from the bathroom already wrapped in his long plaid dressing-gown. The sight of his shins – thin slices of bare male flesh showing between gown and slippers – was a small shock to her, but she acted as if it were nothing. In the bathroom, as she pissed into the WC, pulling pieces of paper from the flowered porcelain holder to wipe herself, she began to daydream. When she noticed her husband's shaving brushes and toothmug by the basin, she felt a rush of sudden pride. Married woman, she thought, rich woman. She thought of the big department stores she'd read about in magazines – thick pile carpets, noiseless lifts, silent, attentive saleswomen in long black skirts. She stood and wiped herself. She might learn to play golf. Sparingly, she applied cold cream to her cheeks then, with a frown, restored the cupid's bow on her upper lip with a touch of lipstick.

Maybe it was not Queenie's fault. No one had prepared her for her wedding night. No one had told her, or talked to her. Queenie was so disdainful, so detached, so in control (so much so, in fact, that June was convinced she had done it already), that no one thought of taking her aside. Not her colleagues, the girls at work, whom she always handled with the most perfect aloof control. No one, and least of all her mother, who should perhaps have thought, but to whom Queenie had long since ceased to grant any daughterly intimacy or affection. I am better than you now, said her daughter's chilly eyes, leave me alone.

So when George plucked tenderly at her nightdress (silk, with a pattern of roses around the bottom, and a ruffle of coffee-coloured lace at the bosom), she shrugged him off immediately. He pawed at her slender shoulder. 'My dear, my dear . . .' he said very quietly, so that his breath – which smelled appallingly of garlic and cheese – grew louder and more intrusive than his voice. It was, of course, the closest Queenie had ever been to a man. She saw the texture of the skin on his face – the circular pores slightly more open around the nose, the small, straight hairs which, as they reached his chin, became the beginnings of his beard.

'Look,' she said, with an expression disconcertingly close to dismay on her face, 'I don't mind if you kiss me. Is that what you want?' She knew about kissing. She'd seen it on the postcards at Skegness. 'Spooning', it was sometimes called. Taken aback, George leaned up on his elbow and looked at her.

'Do you want the light out?' he asked softly. 'Is it the light, love?' He pulled the light switch and that was it. That was the full and dramatic extent of their spoken communication that night.

Now, Queenie's nightdress always did ride up a little, that was true. But when she felt George's rough, hot hand running up over her small, perfect breasts and nipples, she shuddered. She curled herself into a silken ball in the bed and froze. (It has to be said that it was not until a whole week later that George managed at last to get inside his pretty new wife. That night, the night of their wedding, she put up quite a fight.) Her shock and horror at feeling how large his 'thing' had become – as he pressed it, grunting and moaning pathetically, against her thigh under the bedclothes – was only marginally outweighed by her sheer disgust in the morning at finding that he had even made the pale pink sheets wet and slimy with it.

'We are man and wife now,' he muttered, not unkindly, as she emerged from the bathroom next morning and hardly touched her scrambled egg and kidneys. But he sounded fearful, unhappy, unconvinced.

They left for Paris that morning in a rough October wind, with Queenie hardly speaking. Her felt hat was pulled well down over her forehead, and her eyes were hot and angry beneath its stiff mauve rim.

'I've stopped seeing it,' I tell Ede on the phone, 'it's gone away – I mean, I obviously imagined the whole thing. I was in a state, wasn't I?'

There's a pause. I can hear Ede's quick breath as she draws on a cigarette.

'Well, thank God. I was really worried about you. And how's Lenny? He came in yesterday looking really happy, happier than I've ever seen him, in fact. Hope it doesn't kill his art. Are you in love? Can you talk?'

'Not really . . .'

'Which question is that the answer to?'

'Oh, Ede . . .' A brief laugh from her as she accurately reads my sigh. Small limbs struggle somewhere beneath my heart.

Queenie discovered she was pregnant at the Golf Club.

She'd played a good energetic round with Pearl Clark and, feeling a sudden hot dragging in her bowels, she knew all at once that she was going to vomit. She made it to the Club House just in time, but the WC there was dark and cramped, and flecks of vomit splashed out all over her cream and tan golfing shoes. She wiped most of it off with her handkerchief, but she would never get the bits out of the leather fringe. The blasted shoes would have to be thrown out. She drenched herself with Eau de Cologne and sipped a club soda at the bar with Pearl.

When the doctor confirmed that she was expecting, she was pale and grim. It was a cold day in March and she kept her black Persian lambswool coat on in the surgery and shivered.

That's all right, she said, but was there an operation she could have afterwards to make sure she didn't have any more? Money would not be a problem. The doctor patted her knee. You're a married woman, he said, don't make any rash decisions. You go home and look after yourself.

'It had better be a girl,' she told an irritatingly delighted George, 'I couldn't stand a boy.'

*

93

In the dark, he'd come to me. Always, eventually, his shadow in the doorway, mooching across the carpet, as my heart sank. Then sitting, his weight caving the mattress. Goodnight time. He said I was partially responsible for the fact my mother left him – I'd sided with her, been disloyal to him. Rocked the boat, he said. Hadn't behaved like a daughter. I was lucky he still wanted to see me, he said.

I'd acknowledge this stale black responsibility as he lowered his face. I'd smell the sebum on his skin, the dryness of his scalp, the translucent scales of dead flesh flaking on to his collar, the oppressive tang of whisky on his breath. I'd stiffen. I knew that, at fourteen and a half, I was much too old to be kissed goodnight in my bed.

If he just chatted, I was stupidly grateful, glad, I'd answer brightly, full of relief. I'd laugh at something, clinging to the idea that it might be a joke. I'd watch the white moon of his face and hope it wouldn't come any closer, hope he wouldn't kiss my ears, as he did my sisters', who were young enough to like it and giggle.

Before he crept away, he'd look at me hard in the darkness for one more moment. Then I'd be alone, wiping the slug's trail of warm saliva from my cheek, pulling my nightdress down over my knees and thinking I might bring him tea in the morning, like a good daughter.

Later, I go up to the loft with a cup of cocoa, to escape having to sit downstairs with Alistair and my guilt.

'Don't be too late, darling,' he says as I climb the stairs, 'you look tired.'

I nod. It is more than twenty-four hours since I made love with Lenny. I'm ablaze with nerves and energy, light-headed with love. I'm not tired, just taut with anticipation.

I came back yesterday terrified, amazed, ready to confess, to tell him, to turn my life around for the sake of euphoric true love. He was sitting by the fire reading a pile of old Sunday colour supplements, with the sound turned down on the TV, and he looked tired and old and solid after Lenny. 'Al,' I said, 'we have to talk.' But, 'Look in the bedroom,' he smiled, 'see if you like what I've bought.' And I went up and there was this Moses basket on a wooden stand, with blue and candy-coloured rabbit fabric and little bows everywhere. I stood and looked at it and shivered.

'Adorable,' I said, when he came up behind me.

'You look pale,' he said, noticing something.

'Yes,' I said. 'I think I'll go to bed, I feel a bit sick.' And I went to bed – first showering the smell of Lenny from my limbs and hair – but couldn't sleep, and left the light on so he'd know to come up and talk, but he just sat downstairs watching TV and two hours later he was still there and I fell into a dreamless sleep.

Now I cannot think, cannot act. Today, Lenny and I did not sit on our bench, but walked and walked until I had a stitch in my side and then we found an alleyway next to the kitchen entrance of a restaurant, smelling of vegetable peelings and boiled milk. We stood there for a long time, stiff and straight, in each other's arms.

'Oh, God, I've done a terrible thing,' he said, very carefully tucking a strand of my hair behind my ear, 'I've done the thing I didn't want to do. I've made you miserable.' I looked into his face. His skin was so pale that the blue veins stood out – thin rivers of blood flowing to his heart.

'No,' I lied, 'no you haven't. You never could.' All around us, office parties spilled out of restaurants – endless men in suits, with booze-flushed cheeks and tails of Christmas tinsel dangling round their necks.

Delaying, as I nearly always do, the moment when I'll have to paint, I sit and sip my cocoa, eat my biscuit, flicking off the crumbs which settle on the front of my dress, on the slope of the bump.

It's quiet – quieter than usual. Two floors down, the TV is barely audible; all traffic seems to have stopped. I look around me, vaguely expecting to discover the cause of the silence. Is it me, or is the air in the room sucked in, a child holding its breath?

It's very still and very warm.

I finger my paints – Magenta, Ochre, Cadmium, Permanent Rose. When I'm painting properly, when I don't have to think, the colours come mixed straight from my head, burst like lunatics from my hands – dark, bright visions I must put on show. Sometimes I think that's all it is – a straightforward need to be looked at, nothing else – nothing more complex.

But, these last few months, since I've been carrying another body within mine, it's funny how that's changed. Now I paint more slowly, unsure of everything, testing myself, hesitating. The strokes on the canvas are not so much mine, but an interpretation of something I don't entirely understand – not what I would expect. I stare at them, uncertain, unable to compare them with what I did before. And now that I've slept with Lenny, the canvas is bare and hard. A need has disappeared. I force myself to paint, but something else muscles in, tells me I needn't bother: something has been expressed.

I don't want to be looked at.

Now I don't do anything. Now I sit and stare at the tubes of paint. Miles away, an ambulance screams, the sound penetrating the edges of my silence.

I cough, I twist a tendril of hair around my index finger, I lick my lips. The room is lit by two Anglepoise lamps, dating back from the time when we promised we'd fix up something better and then never got around to it. The light for my easel is fine – but the room beyond is in shadow, especially where the roof slopes down to the floor.

I squeeze out black on to the palette. I remember Lenny as he came inside me, his hands upon my thighs, a look of pure, dark concentration on his face. He said he wouldn't do anything, but I begged him. I said I couldn't but he knew. Now it's done and I don't know what I think. I've been unfaithful to my husband in the strict and technical sense; though I know I've already betrayed him countless times on that cold park bench. Well, I've been bobbing along, and now I'm sunk, I've gone down. Sex, actual sex, is, as we all know, the thin line, the dividing line.

I put down the tube and palette and pour water from a plastic jug to stand the brushes in. The sound is clean and startling in the silence. I flex the silky brush heads against the back of my hand. The baby jumps in my pelvis, a small hiccup low in my body.

Then I hear it. A voice behind me, low and distinct, which says, clear as anything, 'You threw my shoes in the river.'

four

'Although sleepwalkers behave like automata, with vacant eyes and a limited repertoire of behaviour, they don't walk about with their hands in front of them.'

'You did. You threw them in the river.' And a hard dragging, a scraping of metal on the wooden floor.

The pain, when it comes, is unexpected and extreme, slicing through my elbow and shoulder, knocking a shock of breath up through my ribs. It's later established that what happened is this: that at the moment of turning, I passed out, and fell hard on the left side of my body, instinctively shielding my belly, which pointed skywards – luckily for the baby cushioned inside. This is Alistair's description anyway.

Mine goes more like this: I hear the voice, low, rasping, angry, and I turn sharply towards him, knocking the water jug as I go, as I fall. At the beginning of my fall I see him standing there about six feet away, gloating – a small boy with a metal calliper on his leg, his face half in shadow. There are three, maybe four, seconds during which our eyes meet, before I hit the floor. Then blackness and wetness – my hair swimming in the spilt water from the jug. That is the end of the fall.

But before I lose consciousness completely, I open my eyes once more and see him standing actually over me. He's scrutinizing me with some hilarity – his eyebrows raised, his mouth mocking, creased with downward lines, his expression no longer young but old and hard. With a small and subtle sense of horror I recognize an adult face, slightly familiar – pasty skull and skin throbbing with a jagged, bloodless pulse. Then I black out.

I have not cried out at all.

'Darling, just a massive thud, that was all I heard. You poor, poor girl . . .'

I am not out for long, and I come to in Alistair's arms, and when I open my eyes the room is – naturally – empty and still, bathed in the acid light of the Anglepoise.

Alistair makes me see the doctor the next day, just to be safe.

'Still kicking?' he asks, pushing the palms of his hands over the live swell of my belly. 'Well,' when I reply in the affirmative, 'that's a nasty bruise you've got, but otherwise all's well – nothing to worry about.'

He turns to the sink to wash his hands, and I can hear his heavy breath. The seat of his trousers is worn and shiny, and there's a patch of sweat in the small of his back, despite the freezing cold day. Behind him, the windowsill is thick with dust.

Unexpectedly, I burst into tears.

'I'm sorry,' I say, vaguely wondering at the fact that his unappealing physical appearance should encourage me to confide in him. I try to explain. 'I think I've been hallucinating,' I tell him, 'I keep seeing something. I'd really like to see someone, a counsellor, or psychiatrist . . . or something.'

Now he's at his desk writing notes. I relax a little, because I've said it. He glances up briefly from the pad. He seems oblivious, his eyes fixed on something beyond me.

'Look, dear,' he says, 'it's quite normal, you know, to be emotional at this time,' and he leans over and pulls down the lower rim of my eyelid from which tears are still springing. He shoves a box of tissues across the desk and says I should see the nurse for a blood test to check for anaemia, but that the main thing is to relax and get plenty of sleep. Then he grabs the next patient's notes.

I walk out without bothering to dry my eyes, and hit the streets which are a circus of litter and grey faces and dog shit. Suddenly it's clear to me that there are no rules. In fact, now I think of it, I don't know why I ever imagined there were. Well fuck that, I think, and hail a cab and give the driver Lenny's address in Kentish Town.

'Hey,' he says.

This time there's no preamble. I take off my coat and my knickers and lie back on his bed and in seconds we are a live mesh of cheeks and lips and arms. I've never been this close to anyone, I think, with an amazement bordering on fear. His pillows smell of warmth and hair and spent matches.

'What happened?' he asks, finally.

'I saw him again, that boy,' I reply. 'Yesterday.'

He's quiet, looking at me, I have no idea what he's thinking. 'You think I'm crazy—' I begin.

'Yes,' he interrupts.

'You do?'

'Beautiful and crazy, like . . .' He leans over and cradles my head in his arms, kisses my temples, my eyelids. This is a joke, I think, suddenly full of anger. I withdraw slightly.

'What's the matter?' he asks immediately.

'This is ridiculous,' I say. How can I inspire passion? My stomach is a map of blue veins, drum-tight, hot, the palms of my hands sticky with a pregnant flush. I'm an animal about to kneel and deliver on a warm bed of hay. My nipples leak colostrum. I want sleep more than sex, food more than love: I can't be sexy. There's a long silence and he turns away, rolls a cigarette, ignores me.

'What can this mean?' he says, from far away. 'You've come to me.'

'Have I?'

The answer hangs in the air between us, a life line. He grabs his end, but I leave mine swinging.

'Well, haven't you?'

He licks the paper and watches me carefully as I swing my legs and ease myself off the bed, clutching my bump with one hand, and progress to the bathroom to pee.

'Please,' I say, in an obviously mean-spirited way, 'please don't try and read something into everything.'

But when I come back into the room, he's quiet, sitting naked on the edge of the bed staring into the fire, little curls of hair on the back of his neck slightly squashed from lying down. I kneel in front of him, with the heat from the fire licking my naked back, and rest my cheek in the furred dip between his thighs.

'I love you,' I say, terribly startled.

Startled to hear myself say the words, and startled because now I know this is how I was always waiting for it to feel with Alistair. Only it never did.

Queenie was up and playing golf only three weeks after the child, a boy, was born. Needless to say, she surrounded herself with the necessary staff: a maternity nurse for the first weeks, with a full-time nursemaid, Deirdre, following swiftly on her heels. The latter was a young rather dim girl from Derby, who smelled of perspiration and bit her nails and never said a word, but Queenie kept out of her way on the whole.

Rather aggravatingly, she'd had to get rid of the house-maid, Violet, who'd stolen a small piece of her jewellery only weeks before the birth, thus inconveniencing the whole household terribly. From then on she'd kept the most valu-able pieces under lock and key at the bank.

They called the boy Douglas.

George had kept himself to himself right up until the boy was born, which suited her. One drinking bout just succeeded another – there was that, and then Queenie also knew he was still seeing that woman at Normanton-on-Soar. Marjorie Lang was a thirty-year-old widow with dull red hair and a mass of pale irregular freckles which spilled on to her hands, her face, her cleavage, as though she'd been sprayed with butterscotch. Pearl said men went for Marjorie, yet neither she nor Queenie could fathom why, what with her pale wishy-washy eyes and trace of an ugly Stoke accent, and the fact that she didn't bother to make up or do anything to her hair. Of medium height, and hardly slender, she had a little money from her marriage but not enough to make a difference. Her clothes were ill fitting and out of date.

'I just can't abide redheads,' Queenie remarked to Pearl, 'ever since I was scratched by the caretaker's ginger tom at school. Haven't been able to trust them since.' Still, George was frequently to be seen drinking cocktails with Marjorie Lang, whilst Queenie perfected her game.

Exactly a year after their marriage, George and Queenie had bought a smart bungalow with a veranda, on the river at Normanton, and they entertained there most weekends through the summer. It was close enough to the Golf Club for Queenie, and George could have a small rowing boat. There was a decent-sized new boathouse, painted green and white and almost hidden by a weeping willow. It was by this boathouse that Queenie first found hard evidence of her husband's affair with Marjorie Lang.

It was not much. Two innocent browning apple cores, flung down in the caked dried mud, one of them smeared with lipstick. That, and the thin tortoiseshell comb that George always kept in his waistcoat pocket. It was a chill late August evening, and Queenie, bulkily pregnant, stood on the river bank, a mauve cashmere cardigan around her shoulders. The air was very still, with an odour of river water and decay. She stood there, unmoving, the handful which confirmed all of her suspicions held out at arm's length in front of her. Two cores in her hand – the flesh bitten away to reveal the pips, and the tough curved membrane which covered them. And the comb, with its fine sharp teeth, caked with debris from her husband's scalp. Queenie froze. The river hissed at her feet.

She was not very surprised. She'd watched him with Marjorie, seen the way he talked to her – too emphatic and concerned, as if she were a child. She'd seen how his fingers drummed the counter impatiently as he ordered her another Dubonnet and lemonade, and his head turned constantly, as if he could not even bear even that short walk to the bar away from her. Pitiful, she'd thought, but she'd felt nothing but a quiet scorn. It hadn't occurred to her to wonder, or to worry. Marjorie's cheeks were fat and her chin was weak, and her brown woollen skirts didn't hang well and were at least two seasons old. Queenie did not rate the surprised, attentive laughter in her face.

All the same, it galled her that she hadn't worked it out for herself. She'd thought it was just a drinking thing, just the Golf Club, nothing more. She licked her lips. Her mouth was dry, her teeth coated with something bitter and metallic which welled up from her gut. The child she carried pummelled at her ribs, gave her constant heartburn, and she twitched irritably. She held the cores for a moment, frowning, then turned and threw them into the darkening water, watching as they bobbed and drowned, as their pallor slid away from her. The comb followed them, and was gone instantly. The high, grey grass on the bank buzzed and shuddered with life. Then, wiping her hands on the haunches of her dress and drawing her cardigan around her, she walked slowly back to the bungalow.

He was dozing in a chair on the veranda. The radio was on, a dance band. Queenie poured herself a Scotch and fetched her pack of bridge cards. Seating herself at the small card table inside, she glanced around her, shuffled and began as usual to play patience. She could observe George easily enough through the open window. River sounds snuck in, and now and then the high-pitched whine of a mosquito. Queenie slapped the cards quickly down on the table, her nails clicking against their shiny backs. She pretended to play patience. But soon her eyes were fixed again on her dozing husband.

It was 10.37 p.m. on 27th August 1923.

Nobody saw her face that evening, and probably she herself was not aware, but for something close to half an hour she sat there, unmoving, in a trance of concentration. Her eyes had the hot lithe look of a person who'd truly like to slice another's skull wide open and spill the gristly, sticky contents over their knees.

Next day I lie and tell the clinic I have a doctor's appointment, and go instead to Lenny, who takes me apart.

He's standing by the window looking at the dying sun, and I'm noticing how gentle and aloof he is, how fragile but combative, like a boy. I take in his shoulders – thin and slightly rounded in his T-shirt, his impossibly babyish white-blond hair straggling with tiny loopy curls round his ears, the surprisingly male curve of his biceps. I think lazily of how I love him, of how, in a sense, he's mine. From somewhere deep in the privacy of this thought, I shift toward him on the bed, rest my chin on my bare arm, and watch him through half-closed eyes. He turns and looks at me without smiling, and I feel a tremor. A dark bubble of expectation under my ribcage. Still he doesn't smile.

'What's the matter?' I ask, suddenly fearful of the answer. He comes over and sits on the bed. His eyes are so black, so filled up with shadow, I can hardly read them in the gloom.

'You,' he says, 'you are. You are the matter.' Then he kisses me, and the kiss is rough and angry. 'Turn out the light,' he says, 'I'm sick of it, I don't want to see.'

'But . . .'

'Turn it out,' he says in a hard voice, and I do, and he pulls me to him. The light outside has almost gone, drained away, leaving the dregs of an opaque and wintry afternoon. 'Susan,' he says, and he lies on me then, pressing me into the pillows, and I feel the hard weight of his arousal. But I cannot stand him on the baby, and have to move him off. 'OK, OK,' he says quietly, and grasps me from behind, and I turn my head to kiss him, but he pushes it round again and yanks my head back by the hair and roughly sticks his fingers in my mouth, at the same time hooking down my knickers and pressing his whole hand in there, into me. I gasp and almost struggle, but realize at the same time that I won't.

When he enters me it's brisk and painful – he drives himself in and out as though he hates me, as though I've brought him to it, but at the same time the pressure of his fingers all over me forces a quick, hot orgasm. I arch my back, surprised, angry, but wanting to go on. He grasps me tighter than ever and lets himself come, then hugs me to him, breathing in my ear.

'You see,' he says after several seconds, whilst my eyes fill involuntarily with tears, 'I'm not what you think. I'm not all that good. You can still go away if you want.'

His voice is bleak and dead. My whole body trembles.

She did not say anything to him. It wasn't necessary. She relished the act of arming herself, the feeling of strategic superiority, far more than she required the emotional satisfaction of confrontation. Above all, she wanted things at her pace. And, anyway, the idea of his straying had always been there and, though it pricked at her pride, there was even an element of convenience. For, eight weeks into pregnancy, and disgusted with the changes sexual intercourse and conception had wrought already on her body, she had removed herself to a separate bedroom, one of the four guest rooms. George had appeared, dismayed, in her doorway once or twice, but she'd quickly had a lock fitted and he'd got the picture. Like many others, this matter was never discussed or referred to by either of them.

She did not say so, but she fully intended to continue to use this as an effective method of contraception, long after this pregnancy was over and done with. It was his fault, anyway, if he would not use a rubber thing.

'Try to focus on the baby, now,' comes the warm steady voice of Myrtle Robinson, 'imagine that you and your baby are one and the same . . .'

In Myrtle's class we relax together. Active birth means being in control, she says, and we'd all agree that we want that. Virgin thin, with a bright hennaed curtain of hair, and an assortment of skimpy cheesecloth shirts which (in stark contrast to the rest of us) highlight her absolute lack of breasts, Myrtle teaches us to breathe in a wide pink room with a landscape of cushions and a pile of winter coats and shoes in the corner. Hard though it is to believe that the pristine circle of her waist ever accommodated a child, she herself gave birth squatting in a special hired pool erected for the purpose in the living-room. Her partner – a faceless, bearded man glued to the TV as we all process heavily past and up the stairs – photographed it and one day the pictures are handed round at the end of class. It looks excruciating, horrific.

'Now relax,' she chants, 'feel the breath, your baby cradled inside you, the tiny heart beating . . .' I try to surrender to the unknown space behind my eyelids, but Lenny's face dives across the blackness again and again. Pulling at my hair. His fingers opening me. Fragility and sex. Half opening my eyes, I stare at the poster of Picasso's *Mother and Child* above the fireplace, its edges curling where the Blu-tac has come unstuck. Fleshy curves, fat beauty. Far away, the Balham night traffic roars. I place my hands on the wide arc of my belly. In the room, someone stirs, someone coughs, someone sighs.

'I am unhappily married.' It has always been there, hovering, but now this unappealing fact swoops down and lands, clearly and heavily, at my feet. 'Here I am,' it says, 'what will you do about me?'

'Now,' says Myrtle, 'open your mind completely. Think of the people you love, of your partner – imagine all the things you'd like to say to them, things you feel and haven't expressed. Let it all out in a long breath . . .'

Nothing. Blank, blank, blank, a blackout. A gap. The faces on the carpet around me are serene, relaxed, open –

embarrassing. You'd think there'd be a sign by now that they'd see I'm not one of them. But there isn't, and my diaphragm lifts up and down and I continue to breathe — fraudulent and unhappy. A haunted woman.

In the loft, a new painting is in progress.

It's nothing like my others — all shrill, sunny landscapes, with childlike figures in the foreground. This one is different. It acknowledges the blank canvas — square and certain — for a start, then breaks it with a band of pure colour. I spent half an hour on a stark December morning mixing this pink and I know it's the right one. Next to that, a band of scarlet, almost as thick, followed by a layer of violet, then yellow, pale as honey. It's hard to put into words, but there's a definite intention in this painting which fills me with hope.

These colours mean no one can touch me.

'I don't know,' says my mother, 'I don't know what to do. She hardly ever phones me and when I try her the answerphone's always on. I feel she's withdrawing from me, my own daughter.'

'It's the money, isn't it?' I say. 'I think in her heart she always wanted the money.'

'Oh, Susan, how can you say that? This is him, he's done this to her . . .'

'Mummy, she's a grown-up, she's twenty-five years old.'

'If you could just make an effort — rise above the situation, talk to her.'

'She won't talk to us, not if we refer to this . . .'

'Oh really! Everything comes back to it, doesn't it? Well, he's got what he wanted, that's all I can say. Well done, Douglas!'

'Oh, I'm sorry . . .' I begin.

'When he died,' she continues, 'I thought, at last, this is the end, it's over . . . but of course it wasn't. I should have known. That evening, the evening they told us he was dead, I wanted to celebrate but I couldn't. I was too frightened. Ken was out and I went around putting on lights. I'd forgotten how frightened I could be. I left the light on all night in the hall.'

'He was a bad man,' I say, 'he was bad to all of us.'

'Oh God. I feel so guilty,' she says. 'Guilty that I married him, guilty that I left. Is it me? Have I done this to us?'

'Mummy, don't,' I say.

'He was a miserable man. He had a terrible childhood. Your grandmother was a cold woman, really brutal, you know. Maybe I should have helped him more — got him proper help, I mean — but he wouldn't have taken it. He had no heart, you know, Susan.'

'He was beyond help.'

'The trouble is, she's getting so like him.'

'She's turning into him.'

'Or them.'

'Them?'

'The two of them. Oh God, I don't know what the balance of power was, but it was always the two of them really, in the end. Him and Queenie.'

The thing is, this painting has come from somewhere else. It's not a controlled act — far from it — it's taken me by surprise.

With Nina Simone turned up loud for my baby, I mix the colours as thickly as I can, jabbing my brush into a red which is defiant and furious, which will break out if it can. Despite the cold weather, I'm perspiring. The tops of my thighs ache with the stretching weight of my child.

I've never been frightened by colours before.

'Couldn't you give the painting a rest, now?' Alistair asks when he sees my hectic face, the shadows under my eyes — when I smash two of our best coffee cups in one day. 'Just until after the birth?'

I hope he can't interpret the impatience, the absolute lack of understanding in my eyes. Ignore him, a nagging voice hisses in my heart, he's not one of us.

Ten days before Christmas, I cut down my hours at the clinic, leaving two days free to rest. I spend them having sex with Lenny.

'You are extraordinary,' he says, his mouth pressed

against my wet and naked buttocks, my parted thighs, his fingers tracing spider paths over my belly, following the baby's rhythmic kicks, 'both of you. I think I've fallen in love with you and the little guy. It won't be the same when he's not inside you any more.'

'How d'you know it's a he?' I ask.

'Oh,' he says, 'I know you. You'd only have boys.'

Alistair pays a surprise visit to the clinic to take me to lunch.

'I had a meeting,' he explains, looking vague and sad, his raincoat over his arm, 'so I thought . . .'

We go to a pasta place in Marylebone Lane, full of families and Christmas shoppers, and eat tagliatelle and wet, wilting salad. I think of Lenny waiting in the Square for me, and notice that an icy rain has begun to fall.

'Well,' Alistair says, wiping the oil from his lips with a badly stained napkin, 'hey, this is nice. A change from sandwiches.' I look at him. He tries, I think. Oh, he's really trying. He deserves better. 'I'm Dreaming of a White Christmas' plays in the background. A baby in a highchair drops peas on the floor.

'So,' he says, at last, frowning, 'so. What is it?'

Oh, I think. Oh, OK. I take a breath.

'Well,' I begin rather brightly, 'it's not working, is it? We're not happy any more, are we, Al?'

He stops eating. He puts down his napkin. He glances

across to check the people at the next table have not heard. He looks absolutely shocked. More shocked, I have to admit, than I would have imagined.

'What on earth are you talking about?' he says. 'Susan, have you gone mad?'

Well, what is there to lose?

'I'm sorry – I'm surprised – if you're shocked, Al, but I think we should separate, at least for a while, at least until I've had this baby. Then maybe we can talk.'

Alistair stares at me for a minute, a horrid, angry, burnt-out stare, and then with sudden decisive efficiency takes up his knife and fork again and continues to eat. He takes a swallow of wine. He shakes his head.

'Ede would have me,' I add more quietly, thinking of Ede, but seeing Lenny's bed.

'Oh no, oh no,' and he does sound properly shocked as he struggles to chew, 'oh no, you're being ridiculous. You don't know what you're saying. I'm sorry, Susan. I'm sorry, but I'm not prepared to have this conversation, not now, when it's so clearly hormonally induced . . .'

'Look, Al . . .' I begin, almost shouting.

He looks around again, as if to gain the support of the whole restaurant or – more likely – because he's embarrassed. Nobody pays any attention. The baby has dropped all the peas and is now flinging teaspoons.

'We're about to have a child, Susan – and I mean "we". "This baby" – for Heaven's sake, you talk as though I'm not involved.'

'But, Alistair...' Words, ideas, my unhappiness is taking an expressible shape at last and he's going to stop me, I know he's going to stop me. Already his steady, knowing face slows me down.

'A colleague's wife went through this, darling,' he insists, more gently now, 'I promise you. They found her wandering in floods of tears in Windsor Great Park. Once she'd had the baby she was fine.' He puts his hand on mine and I remove it, furious as a child. 'You must realize you're under the most tremendous pressure – all the changes and so on. I do understand. And maybe you should have stopped work earlier – not to mention the painting. But we're nearly there now, aren't we?'

I stare, silenced by a slow horror. I don't really listen. Instead, I notice the thin certain line of his mouth cracking his face unattractively when he talks. The knot of his tie at his throat seems suddenly ridiculous, his hair unnecessarily short and black. Why does he groom himself, I wonder to myself? And almost laugh.

'It's chemical, Susan,' he insists, and there's a laborious scientific kindness in his voice, 'your anger. You must realize that? The fact is, you don't know what you're feeling.'

I try to look at him. The song has changed to 'See Amid the Winter's Snow'. Freezing air as the door swings open. Someone arrives at the baby's table and there are greetings and the baby is kissed on the head. For some reason, this – much more than anything Alistair has said – makes me want to cry. Because inside I'm brittle as ice, ragged, taut.

'Certainly, let's talk once our child is born,' he continues, now completely calm, already congratulating himself on this outcome, the skilled avoidance of a crisis. 'Talk to me then – I'll talk as much as you like then, when you're relaxed. But I'm sorry – in your own interests – I think such a discussion is meanwhile quite untenable.'

He looks at me briefly, to ascertain whether it's a success, whether it's worked. I've no idea what he decides. There's a small piece of coriander or something stuck to his lower lip.

'I love you, darling,' he says, feeling for his wallet, 'I love you so much, you know.' Glancing at his watch, signalling for the bill.

'But, Alistair' – one last chance, counting out the words, chucking them at him, hoping – 'I am unhappy . . .' I see myself lying with Lenny, legs, arms, mouth open. Colours spilling out, defining us.

He leans forward with that taking charge look on his face, the look he had the day I met him when I fainted on his office floor.

'Susan,' he says, 'you're pregnant, that's what you are.'

'I don't think I can do this any more,' I tell Lenny, suddenly. 'So much is about to happen.'

I'm living on the edge – the days are sliding into one another, overlapping, so that each one seems shorter and more urgent than the last. In a week or so all our lives will change. Alistair has no idea and neither has Lenny. None of us have any idea. Only my body knows, hugging the smaller one inside it with regular, rhythmic, practice contractions.

'Susan, dear,' says Mrs Hoffman, 'you look horribly pale, you really do. Are you sure you're not overdoing it?'

'I'm not going to have to turn midwife, am I?' laughs Mr Sudbury, coming up and leaning his strong bared forearms on the desk. 'I hope you know what you're doing . . .'

I know what I'm doing. It's just that I never meant to do it. I get up in the dark, groping my way through a space inhabited only by objects, metals and minerals. I stumble along until I find him. We touch, fuck, cry, and the world lights up. My face in the mirror is luminous, my skin and hair, the taste in my mouth, are different when I'm with him, when I've slept with him; I can only eat and talk when he's close. Otherwise the world is dead to me, a place of concrete and ashes. In a strange, unimagined way, I want to die.

'Hush,' says Lenny, gathering my hair in his fingers, 'don't think about it, don't think at all, not right now.'

Then there's a pause and he's turning away. My mouth feels hot, on fire. I want him to grab me, the way he did before, inject me with his darkness, make love something crude and redundant, something we don't need.

'Lenny?' He's motionless. I catch the sleeve of his shirt. It's unbuttoned, so it comes away in my hand, loose, warm fabric, imprinted with his smell.

'I didn't mean to do this to you,' he half sobs and I struggle round so I can see his face, and he's crying like a child, snot running down in two straight, thin lines from his nose, 'I'm sorry,' he says, 'I'm so sorry.'

I put my arms around him and press my face against the nearest bit of him, and it's very odd but in a flash I can see the little boy who carried the remains of his father ashore in an earthenware pot — his chin all brave and set, his mouth all hard, and layers and layers of uncried tears waiting just behind his eyes.

It's almost Christmas.

The boy had a new jersey. A new jersey and new shoes. She'd sent Deirdre into town with him to get the shoes (the contraption on his leg always made fitting a dreadful headache) and now they were back and he was standing in the morning-room wearing them, waiting, apparently, to show her.

'He's ready, Mrs Hancock.' Deirdre put her head around the door in her sloppy, rather aggravating way. 'D'you want to see?'

Queenie made a point of not answering, but twitched her shoulders and smoothed her hair and crossed the hall. It was Saturday morning. Sunlight streamed through the lozenges of stained-glass in the landing window, showing up clouds of dust in a stream of purple light.

'Ah,' she said, puckering her mouth into something like a smile, 'what a very smart little boy . . .'

She walked over to him. He stood, a crabby five-year-old – this pathetic, small version of his pathetic drunken father. A toothy smile, hands clasped.

'New clothes,' she said, and suddenly wanted so much to hit him, to see him flinch. 'Nip for new, nip for new!' she exclaimed, then, and reached out and tweaked his arm between finger and thumb till she felt the flesh compress in her grasp. He burst immediately into shocked tears – a heaving animal noise.

'Mrs Hancock!' cried Deirdre, who was hovering in the doorway, watching. 'Dear, dear, whatever did you do?'

'Oh, don't you know the rhyme?' asked Queenie, slightly flushed from the effort of pinching so hard. ' "A nip for new, Two for blue, Sixteen for bottle green . . ." Don't you know it? I thought you'd know it . . .' And then, 'Silly boy, pull yourself together now,' she said, bending down and making a pretence of hugging him, whilst in fact shaking him by his thin shoulders. 'That's enough now,' she said, more sternly, and turned and left the room before she shook him to death like a terrier shakes a rat.

I dream that Alistair and I are making love and just as he is almost there, the phone begins to ring and I know it's Lenny.

'Leave it,' Alistair whispers, and oh, now we must finish, I must make sure we finish, so I can rush to answer before it stops. Our bodies crash and pound together. It rings and rings. Alistair hurtles on. His eyes are closed, his mouth wide open.

'Come on, come on . . .' I have to get him there. The phone rings and rings. I panic, I struggle to hurry him. I tighten the muscles of my vagina until my whole body is tense with the effort. I try to think of things to say which will bring him off, but 'Come on, come on . . .' is all I can manage. I dig my nails into his buttocks, cup his testicles, touch him in small, secret places.

And then at last something triggers it and he comes in a series of surprised, relieved gasps. His semen is cold as fish. And I slither out from under him and race to the phone and just at the precise second I reach it the line goes dead.

And it's snowing outside – big, drifting flakes – and I press my forehead on the carpet and hope I will die too.

Five days before Christmas, I stop work completely.

'Well, Happy Christmas to you, my dear,' says Mrs Varten. 'Of course we'll all be waiting to hear.'

'Now, I don't want you drinking this now,' says Mrs Hoffman, producing a bottle of champagne from her Vuitton bag, 'it's to wet the baby's head.'

'Oh, you shouldn't,' I say. 'Thank you, you're very kind . . .'

'Take care of yourself.' Mr Sudbury stands awkwardly in the hall and pats my arm. 'I want you back in the spring, you know.' Mr Dean bobs forward and kisses me on the cheek.

'Happy Christmas, and good luck,' they all say, 'promise you'll phone us,' as I walk out on to the chill four o'clock streets, strung with expensive silver-white light.

Again, I am a cheat. It's a false identity, some made-up person they're wishing good luck to, and in a moment I'll round the corner and discard the disguise, leaving it hanging on a parking meter, or neatly folded on the scratched black shelf in some piss-reeking phone box.

My hospital bag is packed and sits on the landing like a time bomb. There's a night shirt, breast pads, sanitary pads, and clothes for the baby, as well as glucose tablets, Calendula cream, and food and drink for Alistair. He's been regrouting the bathroom in the evenings, scraping out all the mouldy black stuff from between the tiles and putting in new, leaving a perfect grid of cream and white.

'I'm going round to Ede's,' I lie on Sunday night, hovering by the laundry basket watching him.

'Sit down,' he says, without looking up, 'why don't you?' He has the radio on. There's a consumer programme about ethical bananas. He's calm, contained. He might suspect something, or not. I've no idea. I can't read him.

'I can't,' I say, terrified he'll make me, 'I must go or I'll be late.'

'OK. See you later.' His voice is subdued, but not unduly so.

I go, because time is running out. Wednesday is Christmas Day. I don't know what will happen after that.

The baby's head's engaged. 'Oh yes, it's well down,' says the midwife, gently pressing with her fingertips, 'all systems go, I'd say. This time next week I'd guess you'll be a mummy . . . A real Christmas baby, eh?'

'I suppose so,' I reply, smiling, and looking shiny and excited and all the things expectant mothers are supposed to look.

Alistair has to work on Monday, so I spend the day in bed with Lenny. We automatically begin to fuck, but our hearts can't do it and in the end we lie there watching kids' TV and feeling miserable. There's a holiday Disney film on about a dog who makes its way back hundreds of miles through the snow against all odds to the people it loves. We sip flat Orangina and I almost cry.

'I feel like that dog,' says Lenny – not really joking – and we lie there together and watch the film which just makes everything seem worse.

*

Queenie began to keep a diary, noting down every little aspect of George's infidelity – his absences, his latenesses, when he'd been drinking. All his misdemeanours in one neat little book with a black tape wound around it. She locked it in her bureau drawer and told no one. It lay there like a secret weapon – a phial of poison, a blade concealed in an umbrella or the heel of a shoe. It might come in handy one day, she thought.

Alistair snaps on the overhead light. Black spots bulge in the corner of my vision. 'Look, excuse me for asking,' he says, 'but where've you been all day, and why are you sitting in the dark?'

'Oh goodness,' I reply. An hour has slipped by. I meant to go upstairs and change, wash, the usual cover-up. Maybe even paint. I began to think, mesmerized by the winking red eye of the answerphone. I didn't even play back the messages. 'I went shopping, just got back – well, an hour ago. I was going up to the loft but I'm so tired.'

Alistair places his briefcase on the table. A cold, creased copy of the *Evening Standard*, his keys. He goes back into the hall. I hear his footsteps on the stairs. The long flush of the lavatory.

'Why don't I believe you?' His voice floats back to me, a broken thing, meaningless and unconnected with anything I know. I rest my head in my hands. 'Why don't I?'

he asks again, more of himself than me. 'God knows, I'd like to, but I don't.'

'Alistair,' I lift my head, 'are you drunk?'

'Not yet,' he replies. And the door slams hard.

But next morning, he's contrite, he kisses me on waking, brushing his fingers down my thighs.

We decorate our tree with red bows and thirty sharp little lights. He spends a long time plugging and unplugging, checking and fiddling with the bulbs until they all work. This process appears intrinsically to cheer him up. When he flicks the switch and they all light up, he throws an arm around my shoulders. 'There!'

I don't know why he's doing it. If the baby doesn't come, we've agreed to spend tomorrow at his mother's house.

'My back aches,' I tell him, later. He's doing the *Times* crossword and eating Bombay mix at the kitchen table.

I stack the dishwasher. The service of nine lessons and carols plays on the radio. Outside it is already less light — the sky, cold and sour all day, is finally giving way to night. A lamp in the street above our kitchen window flickers, falters, and then glows, a steady lozenge of light.

Alistair scoops Bombay mix into the palm of his hand and tosses it back into his mouth, crunching, concentrating.

He clicks the button on the end of the Biro in and out, then taps it against his teeth. I see him as the little boy he must have been – smart and confident at birthday parties, a team leader who could talk to grown-ups, with neat hair, a velvet bow tie on an elastic. First in the queue for a piece of cake to take home. The sort of boy who'd look at me as if I were a lower life form; the sort of boy who made me not want to go to parties.

'Just try and relax, darling,' he says, crunching and clicking away.

It's Christmas Eve.

'I lied,' I told Lenny, lying in his arms three days ago, 'I don't love him. I didn't love him when I said that, I don't think I ever have.'

'You never told me you loved him, Susan,' he said, giving me one of his wild, dark stares.

'I didn't?' I was confused. I wanted him to tell me to leave Alistair. I wanted him to present a solution for me.

'No. But it doesn't matter – if you do.'

'Oh, for fuck's sake, Lenny . . .'

'Don't,' he said, kissing me with tiny, deliberate kisses all along the line of my linea nigra, 'stop assessing. It doesn't matter. Just . . . stop . . . everything.'

I thought of Alistair, of our home together, of the bedroom and the landing and the piles of clothes and bills and magazines and the apricot bathroom with the regrouted tiles and the matching towels and the spider plants. I thought of Lenny's face and body and hands. I thought, well, it's all right for you. Then, angry with myself, I thought: If this is his way, it's working. Freeing me like this draws me to him like a magnet.

'You remind me of a boy I knew when I was a student,' I tell Lenny, 'American too, from Chicago. Eight of us shared a house and it was the middle of a hard winter, and he smoked too much dope and had a terrible cough – he always woke us early in the mornings with his coughing. We only had those Calor gas heaters in the house, and his gas always ran out. One night, it was so cold, he came and slept in my room, on a mattress I had on the floor. We talked for hours about everything, and then I pulled the string of plastic pearls I'd been wearing and they broke and rolled all over the floor. He picked one up and put it in his mouth, and said, "Come and get it, Suze" and I went over and took it in my lips, and we kissed, a long kiss with the pearl in there somewhere still, tiny and hard. We lay and kissed all night until the room was light and freezing and the gas ran out, and then got up and went to our lectures, that was that.'

'What happened to him?' Lenny asks.

'I've no idea. I don't think we ever did it again. It was just one of those things.'

'Why am I like him?'
'I don't know. You just are.'

Now, at last, I go and stand in front of my painting and wonder why I felt so hopeful. I fold my arms and search for clues.

Looking around in the glare of the lamp, I notice that the floor, the windowsill, the mirror, all need a good clean. The baby's gone very quiet. My body's light, the veins on my wrists the brightest electric blue.

Eventually, I switch off the light and go back downstairs.

I try to sip a mug of tea but feel shaky and sick. Small white flakes of snow are just squeezing themselves out of the black night sky.

'It really looks like we're in for a white Christmas up here,' says my mother, 'Ken's just taken the dog out and he says it's settling on the golf course.' She's happier than she's been for a long time, because Penny's agreed to meet her and talk, sometime in the New Year. 'I'm sure I can get through to her, make her see sense,' she says. 'Maybe she's realizing she needs me. I'm her mother, after all . . .'

We're invited next door for drinks and I tell Alistair he should go alone, I don't feel like it.

'I won't be long, then,' he says, putting on a dab of aftershave.

'Be as long as you like,' I say, 'I'm going to bed.' And he gives me a quick look.

'OK,' he says, 'whatever.'

She never knew why she chose his shoes.

They were quite simply the nearest thing – that, she supposed, was it (not that she really cared to question herself to that extent, or indeed at all). She did not lose her temper. It was something altogether different, something entirely and gratifyingly within her control. Quite simply, she wished to see something sink, ruined. She wanted to waste something – preferably George's stupid, smiling head – but if not that, then something else which was required and necessary, something which ought not to be lost.

The shoes were new. Douglas was proud of them in a rather tedious, whining way. The river was a hot brown swell. It was simple as anything. She just picked them up and threw.

The child was beyond belief anyway. How could he have sat there dreaming whilst his father touched up that fat and frowzy woman? How could he just dip his toes and play with his model boats whilst all around him the universe spat and crackled with the current of their sex? Sometimes it was as if, when the calliper was put on his leg that afternoon soon after his third birthday, he'd lost some vital part of his brain – slipped back into a depressed, semi-moronic state. As if he were trying to divine whose fault it was, that his leg buckled and he had a weak heart. Paying her back.

It was a hot brackish afternoon. She'd driven up to the Golf Club for a drink with Pearl, but felt too wretched to stay very long. She had the curse quite badly (ever since Douglas it had been bad) and her belly and bowels ached as black clots of blood like raw liver seeped on to her towel. She sat back and drank a gin. The Club was alive with talk, with chatter.

'Poor old you,' said Pearl. She knew all about Marjorie Lang and didn't have a good word to say for her. But it was all right for Pearl — Pearl could relax. Her husband had been killed in an accident in the South of France many years ago. She'd never have to worry about other women.

Queenie drove back to the bungalow half an hour later, succumbing fast to the idea of bed and a hot-water bottle, something warm on the tearing mass of her womb. But as she rounded the corner by the sycamores, there they were, in the distance, set out for her in tableau form, so she could not miss them. Quietly, she pulled the brake and got out. She did not shut the car door, but let it swing, so that they would not hear her. She watched for a second or two, eyes wide, mouth tight.

The Lang woman sat slumped on the dusty bank, her skirt hitched up as far as it would go. Even as she stared, Queenie noticed with pleasure that her calves were of the thick and shapeless variety, best hidden by golfing slacks. But nothing was hidden, nothing at all. George knelt behind her, both his hands down the front of her dress, in her brassière, her hair undone, her head thrown back against his belly. A few feet away, oblivious as if he were blind, sat Douglas, playing with a wooden boat, trailing his good foot in the shallows.

Queenie walked towards the group, aware of nothing but her fury. Her eyes hurt in the brilliant river light – she saw white spots and black dappled shadows. The grass made her long to sneeze, she had to fight to keep her breath even. The closer she came, still they did not hear her, still they did not stop. She saw George's left hand slide down and rummage between Lang's heavy thighs. 'Ah,' said Lang and still no one turned. Douglas's shoes were next to him on the bank, each grey sock stuffed carefully inside. It was so obvious. It took just a tiny second. By the time she'd picked them up and thrown them and the water had held them for a moment before shuddering and closing over them, she did not know whose face to enjoy first:

Marjorie Lang's, red and shiny, as she clumsily closed her legs and made short clutching movements at her throat with her hand; George's, pregnant with explanation, as he struggled to his feet and began to talk, lamely stammering her name; or Douglas's, whose look of shock and misery was priceless, as he sat, white as a sheet, and told her, 'I've nothing else to put on, Mother.'

As soon as Alistair's gone next door, I dial Lenny's number.

'Happy Christmas,' I say. I hear him swallow.

'What're you doing?'

'Nothing. Going to bed.'

'Where's Alistair?'

'Gone next door for drinks.'

'Left you all alone?'

'Well, I told him to.'

'So.' A pause. 'How's the baby?'

'Fine. Still inside. Hey, it's snowing.'

'Yeah. Nice.'

It should be good, but it's not. Our love no longer works on the phone, we drag each other down, it's worse than if we hadn't spoken at all. We have at least three days to get through without seeing each other – more, if the baby comes on time. The room is very still. In the street, people are calling to one another, laughing; a dog is barking.

When we say goodbye and hang up, I sit for a long time staring at the space around me, and I don't know whether I feel weighed down with sorrow, or light and empty – numb. It is only when I finally stand up that I find that my tights and boots and the seat of my dress, as well as the entire chair seat, are soaking wet.

'So funny!' Granny sat back without a smile, and laughed. 'Such a funny little girl, only about nine years old. Douglas had invited her to tea, you see, but he'd definitely said Thursday. When she arrived instead on Wednesday, I told her she'd got it all wrong and would have to go home . . .'

Granny paused to sip her sherry. We watched, fascinated,

as her long upper lip reached into the ruby liquid like a proboscis. She swallowed, dabbed at the corners of her mouth with creased, liver-spotted fingers.

'But no, she just stood there looking, oh, you know, all upset, and said, "But I put clean knickers on!" ' Granny laughed again. 'You should have seen her little face when I shut the door, it was ever so funny!'

We sat and ate our Kunzle cakes and smiled, and then we asked for the story again and this time we laughed a lot. Daddy laughed too. It was only about twenty years later that, shopping for knickers in the Army & Navy, I suddenly remembered it and felt quite sick.

There's about an inch of powdery snow already on the street, hardly touched by tyres, squeaking under our shoes. The car takes a minute or two to start. Alistair has to get out and scrape the windscreen with his Visa card. I squat, breathing through what are the beginnings of contractions, whilst he clears books and maps and boxes of tissues on to the floor.

'I knew it would be today, you know,' he exclaims, 'I purposely stayed under the limit, just in case . . .'

I ignore him. I can still feel more water or something leaking from between my legs.

'Oh, come on,' I mutter, as another pain makes me move around quickly in the seat, 'please let's go.'

I kneel up on the back seat and hold on, resting my

head on the windowsill in clouds of my own breath. All down the street, partying people are laughing and saying goodbye.

I've dreamed this scene a hundred times, and now reality and the dream merge easily like shards of melting ice on water.

I've dreamed that as we leave the house to drive to the hospital, the body containing my baby goes with Alistair whilst the rest of me stays in the house, watching as order and quiet return. Water still drips from the showerhead, where I attempted a panicky last-minute wash. Damp towels, open books, newspapers, underwear are strewn across the bed. Downstairs, the boiler periodically clicks, the fridge hums. A tulip relaxes and drops a yellow petal on the kitchen table. Otherwise, silence.

Barely visible in the half-light of the landing, a small, spare figure shifts slightly, waiting. And the sound of his calliper bumping, slow and deliberate – almost petulant – against the stair rail, seems both less and more real than all the other, quieter, movements in the house.

That night, he walked in his sleep again.

Deirdre, having heard a noise and found him gone from his bed, searched the whole bungalow, before discovering him fast asleep in his father's rowing boat which was pulled up on the sandy soil at the bottom of the lawn. Queenie was woken from the deepest part of her night by Deirdre in tears saying she couldn't rouse him and didn't know what to do.

Pale with anger, shrugging on a robe, Queenie followed the girl out into the blackness. The last phase of night had begun and, though the sky was at its very darkest, one or two birds were just beginning to call. A band of grey hung over the river.

'If you wish to divorce me, Queenie,' George had said, earlier, his voice all tight with reason and calm, 'I understand, I'll make it easy.' Easy for him, maybe, but not for her. She was not going to make his life that neat and simple. Queenie thought of her bridge-playing friends, of the people at the Golf Club, of how divorced people were tolerated but always the subject of secret pity and scorn. She had too much pride, she'd come too far (well, she'd more or less cut herself off from her family when she'd married George), she could not bear it. She was not sure, either, how the money side would work out, and she knew herself well enough to know she could not stand to have a penny less than she already had. On the other hand, it maybe would be worth talking to a solicitor and finding out exactly what her position would be. Meanwhile, she kept on with her diary, itemizing and recording everything, letting nothing go.

'What'll we do, Mrs Hancock? I don't think we should wake him, he might be upset . . .' breathed Deirdre at her elbow. Queenie licked her lips. Her teeth were still furred, her breath rotten, with sleep. A heavy dew was already soaking her feet in their thin slippers. Oh hell, she'd had enough. She stepped forward.

'Douglas!' she tried to shout, but her voice cracked, she was too tired. Goose pimples crept up her arms and legs. Then, 'Oh for goodness' sake,' she said, and, bending forward, grabbed the side of the boat and tipped it neatly over so that her small son rolled out on to the damp stony ground. Deirdre made a noise of surprise and rushed forward to pick him up, but it was too late because he'd already begun to scream. The scream was beyond anything Queenie had ever heard, a scream of horror, live and rigid. He screamed for a full twenty minutes before Deirdre succeeded in quieting him, but Queenie didn't wait to hear it because, her job done (well, she'd woken him, hadn't she?), she crossed the lawn and went wearily back to bed, full of equal hatred for her husband and her son.

In fact, he walked in his sleep on and off for the next six months. Usually, he'd be looking for something, searching inside and under things, muttering under his breath with half-closed eyes, dragging his calliper along in a pitiful way, until he finally came to rest somewhere strange and was often not found till the morning. In a funny way, they got almost used to it. Usually, it was Deirdre who found him. He'd be curled at the foot of the stairs, outside his mother's room, or maybe on the green velvet ottoman on the landing.

sleepwalking

Once, they even found him asleep on the highest shelf
of a bookcase in the study, some five or six feet off the
ground, wedged between George's fishing books and the
Bible.

five

*'The sleepwalker's eyes are unseeing and it is usually dark.
So how does the child avoid walking into things?'*

Jack is born at 8.37 a.m. on Christmas morning.

All night I hang there, on the grey metal hospital bed-head, seeing only Alistair's suddenly alien knuckles, inter-mittently white with my grip, the black mouthpiece for gas and air. Beyond these things, nothing but female, animal panic. I try to breathe. Sometimes I think of Myrtle, see her perfect, thin calm as she squatted before us. I don't think of Lenny at all. It's just as I expected, as I knew it would be: another place, the edge of somewhere else. Then, in the middle of the dark, just when I've more or less given in and learned to die, there it is, a shining second, a slipping, a release, and my baby's coming towards me, through me, out of me, with a wail which must be made of my own breath. 'Well done, you've got a boy,' someone says, 'a lovely little boy.'

'Thank God,' says someone else, possibly Alistair. There's a sudden smell of antiseptic and blood and magically, emphatically, the pain drops away, and I laugh and hold out my arms and the moment is frozen for ever in a special irretrievable place, somewhere between life and death.

'Well done, lovey, all over now,' says the midwife, quickly replacing the sodden scarlet pad under my buttocks with a clean one. She's been with me for hours – a soft, faceless voice, a pair of elbows – and now I notice her, the arch of her eyebrows, the clean, surprising line of her cheek. Another midwife comes in and checks my pulse.

'Happy Christmas,' she says, 'congratulations.'

There's a piece of tinsel in her hair. My baby is wrapped tightly in a towel. Sitting up on the delivery bed, I hold the small new body against mine. It smells of salt, of my own hot insides – familiar and yeasty and alive. I look up, and outside the sun's coming up, and there's an intense and noticeable stillness because it's Christmas Day. Church bells begin to ring. I kiss the wet head, the blood-matted, blue-black hair, the perfect shoulders still smeared with cheesy white vernix.

'Clever girl,' says Alistair, 'I knew you'd do it.' Someone has handed him a polystyrene cup of tea, and he's concentrating on it, and I notice that he's shaky and white and unshaven.

'Oh, Al,' I say. And genuinely try to feel a pang of love for him.

Queenie's marriage was, of course, as good as over. She knew that, he knew that. So it was without any real concern that she sat waiting in the private hospital waiting-room whilst George underwent some tests. She sat, legs crossed at the ankles, her black Persian wool coat drawn up to her chin, picking at the cuticles of her nails.

George emerged at last from under the black and white signs, pale and puffy-eyed.

'We can go home,' he told her, offering his arm, 'got to wait till the beginning of next week, apparently.' His tone was baffled, weary. He looked much older than his thirty-five years, Queenie thought, pulling away in distaste, but nevertheless maintaining her position at his side, like a wife.

At home they found Douglas, waiting alone at the foot of the stairs.

'Deirdre didn't come,' he whined, picking at the scabs on his knees. She was supposed to have given him lunch.

'Oh well,' Queenie shrugged, on her way up to change, 'go and wait in the kitchen and maybe she'll turn up.' Really, anything, to stop him hanging around all forlorn and accusing like that. In her room, she sat motionless at her dressing-table for a long time, and then powdered her nose.

When George was diagnosed a week later as having a cirrhosis of the liver, she was elated, reprieved. She hadn't expected to be a widow so soon. She had in fact been on the verge of filing for a divorce, but she quickly put it on hold and employed a live-in nurse instead. Widowhood would be easy to live down at the Golf Club – an almost pleasant attention, in fact. And there was the added bonus in that, once George was bedridden (which the doctor euphemistically warned her he almost certainly would be), she would be able to make sure that not a single one of Marjorie Lang's communications reached him.

For the first time in ages, Queenie looked out of her window and noticed the flowers, the trees, the sky.

At home a few days later, the families gather round. Champagne is sipped. Hyacinths and lilies pour into the air. It's a real white Christmas, and sun spills, bright as a beaker of orange juice, over the perfect caked rooftops. There's purity in the air; London looks almost clean.

My milk comes in and my breasts are impossibly swollen, cartoons of themselves, barely contained in the rigid confines of my feeding bra. Jack feeds constantly, sometimes every half-hour, leaving only a space to take a shower or drink a cup of tea. In between, I walk around, I look in the bathroom mirror, marvel at the rest of my new self, so separate and small. So empty. I wonder how long it will take for my belly to be taut and firm again.

I don't think about Lenny.

'He's fabulous,' whispers Sara, holding the white sausage of cellular blanket as if it might snap in two, 'did he really come out of my very own sister?'

My mother talks very fast about nothing in particular, uneasy, upset, holding her new status at arm's length, and then succumbs – swiftly, suddenly – and holds Jack tight and weeps a little.

'I'm sorry,' she says, 'but it's the terrible situation. I gave birth to you three, you see, just like this, and watching him split you, it breaks me up, it really does.'

'Your mother's been very down, Susan,' Ken explains kindly, mildly uncomfortable at finding himself in our bedroom, still wearing his padded outdoor jacket, clinking his car keys in his pocket. 'She's in an impossible situation, you know . . .'

Penny does not come round, but sends a gift – a musical mobile of small bears, each with a blue satin necktie, who drift, smiling, round to the tune of 'The Teddy Bears' Picnic'.

'They're fine – everything's just grand,' says Alistair to yet another friend, holding the mobile phone between his ear and shoulder, gathering empty glasses and ribbons and cards on to a tray.

Jack sleeps through almost all of this, waking only to feed, otherwise a perfect small curled human – arms flung wide, fingers spread in the air, as if he fell fast asleep in the middle of making a very important point.

'This,' said our father, opening a briefcase and spreading typed sheets before us on the kitchen table, 'is an affidavit. It has your mother's signature on it. Read it. I think it only fair that you three should know what she's admitted to – her adultery is here, in all its smutty detail.'

We were eating purple Slush Puppies, our lips stained mauve, melting ice oozing from plastic. Daddy fetched us beakers to put them in, and we wiped our fingers, so we could look properly at the papers. We were really embarrassed, we pretended to look closely. There were words like 'intimate' and 'intercourse', and of course we knew what that meant.

'As you will see from the document,' said Daddy, stirring two heaped spoonfuls of Demerara sugar into his coffee, 'she was unfaithful from the word go. Her sexual appetite is simply colossal. She and your beloved 'Uncle' Ray could not contain themselves. In fact, I can tell you that he had his hands in her knickers on the first night they met, at a barn dance. I really do wonder,' he added, laying the spoon on the Formica table, so it left a smeary trail of coffee on the otherwise spotless table, 'what you three girls will make of all this . . .'

I am watched. Every minute of the day, I am looked after. Alistair has taken a fortnight's holiday from the office. I cannot ring Lenny, cannot see him, though Ede has of course told him.

'He sends his love. He says he loves you. God,' she whispers, when Alistair's downstairs fetching tea and Christmas cake, 'I feel bloody treacherous, you know. I'm not sure whose side I'm on.'

I hold Jack against my shoulder, gently bringing up a burp. I sniff the scent of his fuzzy hair, his ear. Such riches. 'I'm sorry,' I say, 'I know.'

'What're you going to do?'

'I don't know,' I reply, as Jack turns his head from side to side, rooting, searching hopelessly for a nipple on my neck, 'perhaps it will all go away.'

'D'you want it to?'

'No.'

'You love him?'

'How can I do this to them, Ede?'

I meant all of them, Lenny too. I don't know who he is any more. I suppose I think we're a family, Alistair and Jack and me. Jack's only five days old and already Alistair's photographed him from every angle – eyes open, closed, half-closed, dressed, undressed, unsuspecting. I expect too much from people, I know – I'm haunted by possibilities. The truth is, I'm not sure I love anyone any more, except Jack – and every photograph makes me more uneasy, plants me more firmly here in this particular space, this scene. As if with every click of the shutter, Alistair directs the light on to the three of us, actively blots out the rest.

I haven't been out of the house in what seems like a very long time so, on the morning of New Year's Eve, I persuade Alistair that Jack and I should go to Mothercare to buy more Babygros and nappies and so on. I'll be fine, I tell him, doing up Jack's poppers for the fifth time in as many hours – we can try out the car seat, and I'll take the sling to carry him in.

sleepwalking

'I don't know, I really think I should come with you,' Alistair frowns, scratching the stubble he always grows on holiday. 'I'm sure you shouldn't be going out, not quite yet, I mean, it's barely a week.'

'Oh, for God's sake,' I say, petrified that he will decide to come, 'it's only a bit of shopping – I want to walk around a bit on my own. I'm going mad, trapped at home all the time. It'll do me good. Please, Al.'

I pause, suddenly struck by the urgency in my voice, the quite blatant need to escape. Alistair takes Jack for a moment, hands me my coat in silence. We don't look at each other. I pick up the baby seat.

'You're not trapped,' he says quietly, biting his lip, 'I care for you, Susan. It's as simple as that.'

'I'm sorry, I'm sorry,' I mutter, but I can hardly be bothered even to be plausible. 'I just need to get out, that's all.'

We go out into the street. The air is a shock, live and cold and stinging. Alistair fixes the seat into the car, then puts Jack in, fastening his little straps in front of his chest, arranging his floppy newborn head against the support cushion. We stand by the car for a moment and look at each other. He hands me the keys, his eyes still angry.

'Hey,' I smile, 'you can read the paper, relax . . .'

'Yeah,' he says, and turns and goes quickly. I watch his head disappear behind the privet. Jack struggles in his seat, impatient, wondering. Just like me.

It's a dry winter morning – the very edge of the year –

no sun, but stark trees and flocks of birds, airborne patterns of black against the chill sky. I drive to the end of our road and turn left. I will go to Mothercare, but instead of going to Victoria as Alistair expects, I drive to the Kilburn branch.

I arrive at Lenny's door with two pale striped plastic carrier bags and Jack asleep in his sling on my breast.

'Oh God,' he says, and then a motorbike goes by and drowns the rest. Inside, we're tentative and slow. It's been more than a week. I can't imagine how I ever dared throw my arms around him. My body's forgotten everything.

'Let me see,' he comes over, so close I can smell his hair and the layer of warmth between his skin and his shirt, and with one finger lifts the flap of fabric which hides Jack's sleeping face. 'Oh, but he's real tiny, Suze . . .' He strokes the cheek, small and rounded as a peach or plum, already pimpled with milk spots, then he looks at me and strokes mine, and I recall with a dim surprise how my body changes when he touches me, how a pleasant weight settles on my solar plexus.

We sit together on the sofa and I undo the clip and carefully remove Jack, still asleep, and lay him on the floor, still in the sling, the helpless curve of his legs sticking through the fabric holes. We hold one another in silence, and we kiss, and I'm shy even of the noise of our lips. Gently, Lenny explores my new body – my belly, shrunk and soft, my large and important breasts, my hands which smell of bed and birth and babies.

'Oh God, I've missed you,' he whispers. Every utterance, every bit of dialogue between us has to be a cliché now, the obvious, the said. There's nothing else left for us — just the inevitable used-up language of people who are secretly sleeping together. For that is all we're doing, I keep reminding myself, just having an affair. In fact, we're better off with silence. I fear for us less, then. 'It's utterly weird,' he laughs, wrapping his arms around me, looping my hair back behind my ears, 'to hold only you without him, you know . . .'

I'm wearing a scarlet flannel dress which buttons up the front for breastfeeding, and Lenny, watching my face, begins to unbutton it. On the floor, Jack stirs and stretches a tiny hand in the air, and I freeze, waiting for the cry. It doesn't come.

'I ought to go, really,' I say. Lenny explores my face, the bones of my temples, the soft spaces in between, presses his lips on my eyelids, whilst still unbuttoning my dress. Gently, he pushes a finger into my mouth. I suck, tentatively, tasting tea and paint and soap, all the sweet, ordinary places his fingers have been.

'Oh,' I begin, but he ignores me.

'I have this little fantasy,' he says, 'that you come and live with me, the two of you. I'd look after you, you know.' The words send a shiver of warmth, a thrill, over my scalp. His finger still in my mouth, running gently along my gums, I stop and look at him. I remember Alistair and his camera — rolls and rolls of film of all of us smiling over Jack. Jack's family — the one he's entitled to. Gently, I push

Lenny out of me. 'You don't know what you're saying.'

'Who says I don't?'

'A newborn baby? Sleepless nights?'

I am half joking. But he doesn't smile, and he looks more serious in fact than I ever imagined. He gives me a despising look, level, right into my eyes, full of pain.

'My nights are sleepless anyhow, Susan. I mean, what d'you expect?'

Small tears creep down my face. Milk seeps out of my nipples into my breast pads. I leak all over, in fact.

Lenny strokes me, goes down as far as my knickers — maternity knickers with a pad. I put my hand on his.

'I have some stitches,' I tell him, 'and I'm still bleeding.' But he takes me in his arms and kisses my face and says it again and again:

'I'd look after you, I want to look after you . . .' And then Jack wakes with a little volley of cries and must be fed.

Once our mother had left, our father still took us every year to the same place in Suffolk for our holidays — partly to rub it in, and partly because he knew nowhere else.

'My wife left me last year,' he told the Howells, who owned the hotel, with the three of us standing there in the vast dark hall in our T-shirts and shorts. 'She committed adultery with a neighbour. I had no idea at the time of course. I'm still taking pills to get over it.' They didn't know how to take it. They were sorting out orders for packed lunches. They narrowed their eyes and disappeared into the adjoining office.

He told the same story to guests in the TV lounge after dinner. They listened and looked at him and nodded at us and sometimes gave us mints off the coffee tray. To begin with, that first summer, he'd show complete strangers the photographs of the family we used to be, but eventually as he got angrier he stopped bothering. One day he sat down and scribbled on our mother's face with red Biro, and then finally just chucked all the photos away.

The last couple of years we went there, he was much less sociable and spent most evenings sitting on the bed in his room drinking Scotch and watching a portable TV, whilst we ran wild in the grounds.

It was a country house hotel. In the brochure it said it welcomed children and dogs, but in fact it was just scruffy and would welcome anything. We went there ten summers in a row. The carpets were full of fleas, our mother said, and Sara once came back with hair lice. There was a mynah bird in the hall and a peacock in the garden and a pet lamb. Often there were ducklings in the airing cupboards in the bathrooms.

In the extensive grounds, close to the woods, there was a summer house, perfect and slimy and forgotten, enclosed by blue cedars. Inside, there was a mildewed pile of *Penthouse* magazines. The first year, we looked at them and laughed, but eventually they were too damp for the pages to turn properly. But every summer we played there with Juliet, the Howells' daughter. Sometimes at dusk we tried to catch bats with our small green fishing nets. We had a special club and invented a secret language.

Then one year Juliet – who was about thirteen – wouldn't play with us any more, and we found her in the summer house kissing one of the cooks, a thin Glaswegian who smoked roll-ups. He laughed, but she slammed the door and told us to mind our own business, and the following summer when we came she had a small baby and was waiting at table. Late at night, we often heard her shouting at her parents. Then doors banging. We never spoke to her properly again.

We had a nearby beach almost to ourselves, because you had to walk across fields to get there. With our mother, we used to walk the whole way – about a mile and a half – but our father, who hated walking, always cheated and drove up as far as he possibly could, parking right up close to the farm gate, where the road petered out and became a rutty track. He then grudgingly walked the rest.

The path was full of clues: as you got closer, sea lavender kissed your feet. Sara, Penny and I lived for the moment when the slice of blue appeared over the dunes and we could shout: 'The sea!'

'It's a nudist beach,' our father pretended, 'we could be in the South of France,' and he insisted upon stripping off and wearing no trunks even though we were embarrassed and always wore swimsuits and changed under our towels.

'It's entirely up to you,' he shrugged, peeling off his underpants, and ripping open the bag of sandwiches, 'nobody's going to force you.'

Ham and tongue and hard-boiled eggs and the colourless flesh of his cock lolling there, half on his thigh, half on the towel. That's what those summers were mostly about, once our mother had left.

As well as the sea there were two lakes, one salt and one fresh water. They were separated from the shingle beach by a row of sand dunes stretching along as far as you could see, towards Yarmouth. The grey-green of the dunes was interrupted only by the jagged corners of cement pillboxes left over from the war, slipping, bleak and sinister with their tiny slit windows, down the steep banks into the lakes.

Daddy used to make bets with us. He offered a prize – one of the felt mice we all craved from the craft shop in Southwold – to anyone who'd swim across the salt water lake with him. I felt sick at the idea. I knew that bodies of dead soldiers probably lurked down there, their black boots bound by weeds, faces pale and sloppy with decay.

'Come on,' Daddy said, rubbing the sand off his hands, 'a mouse for the girl who does it. Sara? Pen?'

'Don't,' I said. I knew our mother wouldn't like it.

But he gave me a terrible look and they got into the lake.

It took less than five minutes to swim across. I sat on a towel and watched them go, moving over the still, scummy surface of the water. A minute passed, I could hear their voices drifting in the heat and silence. I heard his strong strokes as he swam, as he breathed, and their questions, quick, excited. The sun came out and the sky glowed with light, and then it was in again and the dunes were in shadow, the water dark, fragmented.

Resting my head on my knees, I tried to disappear. I heard the far-away sound of water being moved.

When they came running round to tell me they'd done it, they were laughing and dripping and shivering and talking about the mouse he'd buy. He followed behind, slow, naked. He dried himself carefully, not really looking at me.

Later that afternoon I went off alone for a hot silent walk through the dunes and saw two horrid things. A nylon bra, high-heeled shoes, a dirty sanitary towel flung behind one of the pillboxes. And a poor grey rabbit dying of myxomatosis on one of the paths, its visible eye a seething mess of blood and insects.

I don't know, to begin with, what's got into me. Or maybe I don't know that anything has. I don't know how it should be. I have nothing, after all, to compare it with. It only dawns on me creepingly, if at all. Maybe it's true for everyone. I don't know. Anyway.

I sleep when Jack sleeps. I wash and dress myself. I feed him, hold him, change his nappies on the changing table which Alistair has set up in the bathroom. I sing rhymes and songs and talk to him and kiss the warmth of his small head over and over again, on the tender place where the bones of his skull haven't yet fused together. I clean every fold and crease of his body with almond oil and cotton wool; all day I smell the sweet smell of his piss, his shit.

I hang a mobile of ducks and chickens above his cot. When his eyes are open, I realize, with a tight feeling in my throat, that the look is love. Every day, the midwives come and check my pulse with cool, clean hands, then weigh Jack and check the stump of his umbilical cord which eventually drops off, as if he's a small and perfect piece of fruit I've pulled from some tree.

I have to keep the house going, of course. I load and unload the dishwasher, empty the washing machine, hang endless Babygros and muslins to dry against the kitchen radiator. I eat simple, repetitive meals in front of the TV with Alistair, one of us pushing the pram backwards and forwards with a foot.

Alistair is extremely solicitous, but grey faced and tired, except when people are round, when he tidies up and metamorphoses into something proud and happy. At night, I sleep, curled, next to him, his hand upon my bottom, the baby a spot of warmth between me and the wall. It's January.

On the tenth day, the midwives come for the last time. 'Well, good luck,' they say, 'see you at the clinic.' I see them off, smiling, with Jack cradled in the crook of my arm, and feel utterly bereft. Eventually, all the perfect blue and white bouquets are dead. Alistair goes round dropping them into a black garbage bag, and I pour brown foul-smelling water down the sink.

'Back to normal, then . . .' he remarks, as he ties the two ears of the bag firmly together.

'Yes,' I reply, staring at his broad and busy, navy sweat-shirted shoulders.

'Ah, come on, Suze.' He gives me a rough squeeze which is supposed to be affectionate.

Well. The snow's just about all gone, except for a dirty bird-pecked patch or two on a garden wall or the roof of an abandoned car, but it's dark and freezing all day and finally Alistair goes back to work. My brain is hollow, a black hole. I know what I must do, but somehow I manage to put it off.

Then our boiler breaks down, so we have no central heating for a couple of days. Jack and I live in front of an electric bar heater in the sitting-room. He wears a vest, stretchsuit, cardigan, mittens, and four blankets; I huddle under a rug. I watch morning TV, lunchtime TV, afternoon soaps, Oprah Winfrey. Her theme is 'hurting the one you love'. She brings all the men who have ever cheated on their wives into the studio to talk to them about it in front of a studio audience. It's like some imagined confessional hell; it gets everyone nowhere. Oprah wears six silver brace-lets, and touches people on the wrist and says thank you so much for sharing this. I watch until my head could cave in under the weight of the faces and eyes and teeth. I know what I must do. Eventually, the waiting becomes the worst part – an intolerable sentence, a reminder. So at last, blind with crying, I ring him.

'I can't see you any more,' I say, steady-voiced, believable. 'I don't know what you're expecting, but it isn't fair on the baby.' I fix my eyes on Jack, who lies on his side, one thumb in his mouth, the other hand grasping the edge of the Moses basket. He says nothing. I hear his quick breath, then, 'I knew this would happen.'

'Yes.'

'What's the matter?' What does he mean, what's the matter?

'Nothing. Nothing's the matter, Lenny, it's just this won't do.'

My voice is quiet and controlled. He would not know there are tears pouring down like rain. My teeth are chattering, but I hold the phone away from my mouth so he can't hear that either. I'm being wonderful in fact, much better than I could have guessed.

'It isn't fair,' I repeat, clinging to this, 'it's just not fair on anyone, on any of us . . . I have to think of Jack, now.'

Then, 'Well, I'm in love with you, Susan,' he says quietly. 'You know that. I love you and your child. What do you want me to do? What shall I do that is different? Tell me and I'll do it. Actually I'll do anything. I love you.'

'No,' I almost shout, 'there's nothing. Nothing. There's nothing you can do.' I look at the telephone receiver with a sense of wonder, as if it's somebody else's, not mine – something I've picked up off the street and should return or hand in. 'That's what I'm saying – it's hopeless. You know it's hopeless. You've offered me everything you can ... it's my fault, I know. Let's leave it, now. Please, Lenny, this is my fault.'

I scream the last bit and hang up, then take the phone off the hook and breathe. As I cut off the connection, Lenny dies for me, it's done – strangely quick and easy, like cutting off a limb, only to find it was not joined to the central nervous system after all. Well, thank God, I think, surprised and glad. Perhaps I didn't love him very much after all, if it was so easily done. I just couldn't be with him, couldn't be without him. It was all very complicated and wrong.

I exhale slowly. I see that I'm shaking. 'Well, I've done it, I've done it' – I say this aloud, without thinking – to the room, to whoever.

And then – oh shock – a light bulb expires with a sudden ping and there's a low child's laugh somewhere, and I sit for a few seconds in total terror.

George was taking a long time to die, longer than the doctors had implied. Spring came and he was still there, a lot thinner and more or less confined to bed – but sometimes he'd even ask to be brought downstairs, wrapped in a dressing-gown and muffler, and watch Douglas shooting at sparrows in the garden with his peashooter. He'd never come off the booze completely, so he still had his flask of whisky, which the doctors now said could do no harm (though the expense alone annoyed Queenie no end). She was out a lot, playing bridge and golf, as before. She spoke to him no more than was necessary. It was a cold and drearily prolonged situation, she thought, one she'd rather avoid. He knew she was waiting. And she knew that he knew.

And so at this stage it was he who watched her, not the other way round. In a sense, therefore, he had the upper hand.

In fact, he was back straight after the birth. He is without remorse. He gave me no time at all. He was there, waiting, on that very first day, when Alistair brought us home from hospital.

I climbed the stairs and put Jack on the bed in his Moses basket and went to the bathroom and turned on the tap to wash my hands. It was four o'clock in the middle of winter and almost dark. I didn't bother with the bathroom light – there was enough light from the bedroom. I waited for the water to run warm. I yawned and looked around and there he was staring in through the window – not possible of course because it's the first floor, and there's no ledge or anything, but there he was. I froze and he smiled and, with exaggerated slowness, mouthed some words at me. He pressed his face against the glass as real children do, and I saw the blurry fuzz of his breath. He stayed there for perhaps five seconds, then disappeared.

'Al!' I screamed down the stairs. 'Alistair, come here, I just saw him!' I began to shiver and cry.

'Oh really, not that again,' he said, trying to be patient. 'Jesus, I really thought you'd given up on that one ages ago, Suze . . .'

'But . . .'

'Look,' he said, folding his arms and looking hard at me, 'we don't believe in ghosts or the supernatural or whatever, do we? It's in your head, Susan. You gave birth forty-eight hours ago. You're in a fragile state. Relax, darling, don't think about it. Lighten up. My God, look at you, you're all tensed up.' He poured me tea and settled Jack and me in bed, and that was that. He wouldn't listen, and who could blame him, in a way?

A day or two went by, and I knew he was still somewhere around, waiting. And then I started coming in on him in rooms. Anywhere – the bedroom, the kitchen, the hall. I'd round the corner and he'd be standing there, challenging me, unmoving, eyes narrowed and accusing, before he'd fade. I saw his face, briefly, everywhere – in mirrors, in windows, in saucepans, in the dull shine of the TV screen.

For some reason which made no particular sense either then or now, I began to assume responsibility for it, to blame myself. It's not that I doubted the reality of what I saw, I didn't think I was imagining it. But if I really was haunted, trapped in this vision, I'd somehow brought it on myself and so a sense of outrage was pointless. As a result, I rapidly reached in those few days a kind of plateau of isolation, disguising itself hopefully as normality, and found myself unable to share it with anyone, not even Ede or Lenny. I became, I suppose, very depressed, overwhelmed with thoughts of death. Every day, life seemed more fragile and haphazard, decay more solid and inevitable. I watched Jack feeding, sleeping, crying, and was struck with the enormity of what I'd made, what I'd done. My love for him was more than I could bear. It terrified me. If I were to lose him I knew I'd want to break, pierce, shatter myself. I began to suffocate under the weight of whatever bad thing it was that I expected now. I never wanted this, I told myself.

That's when I rang Lenny and ended it.

And anyway, though I'd never really consciously worked it out, I knew now. I couldn't turn away any longer. Past, present and future had combined and the mixture was eating me, blurring my edges, painful and quick as acid.

'I'm not much of a cook,' Granny always told us, 'because I was used to servants. And anyway, I've a sweet tooth — I'm much keener on sweet than savoury.'

For lunch she always made us soup and cheese — Campbell's condensed mushroom soup and Kraft cheese slices, thin as plastic, wedged in the softest of white rolls bought at the post office in Lowdham. Apart from that, her cupboards were cool Formica shrines to violet cremes and truffles and Dubonnet and marzipan cakes. She ate so much sugar, it was like a fairy tale. We asked her once if she believed in fairies. She bit her tongue between her false teeth and looked out of the window, at the children catching her shrubbery with their wheels as they cycled past. 'Maybe I do, maybe I don't,' was the unhelpful reply, rapping on the window at the kids.

She read the *Financial Times* every day to check on her stocks and shares, cutting the relevant columns out with nail scissors and Sellotaping them to the inside of the cupboard where she kept the carpet sweeper.

She was always old, the whole time we knew her — almost eighty when I was ten — and she already had a hearing aid, a wig, and false teeth, as well as great wedges of chiropodist's felt and foam inserted in her shoes for her bunions. She kept these wedges on her bedside table, next to a plastic screw-top jar of Fruit Pastilles, and a frosted pot of Elizabeth Arden face cream.

I didn't love her in any real way — she was never very real to me, an artificial person comprised of mysterious appendages, someone we whispered about before we fell asleep. We often stayed the night at her house and she'd let us go through her drawers, looking at her things. But this was as far as she ever went — she didn't offer any other sort of love. She never hugged or kissed us, though she always made a point of introducing us ('my son's three girls') in shops.

She stopped seeing us the day our father did and we never heard from her again. When I try and think of her, it is still her drawers, her possessions, which stand out.

For instance: she was the first person in the town, so it was said, to have a fibre-optic lamp. We knew this because they were only available at one department store, and the man who sold it to her assured her it was the very first. When we came round, she plugged it in and we sat and watched as peacock blue turned to violet, gold to tangerine.

'Smart, isn't it?' she said, going into the hall to pick up the *Evening Post*. She showed it off for a while but eventually moved it to the spare room as she found it too distracting in the same room as the television.

Less exotic, but a highlight to us all the same, was her kitchen drawer. Standing on a stool you could go through it, taking everything out. It was so dirty, so full of unnecessary, unexplored things. For a start, the lining paper — waxy yellow with a pattern of black snowflakes — crumbs and fluff stood out on it in jagged relief, and it generated the conflicting odours of old butter and dog biscuits.

It wasn't just full of knives and forks, but contained a great many things — all chewed or broken or soiled or all three. Kitchen scissors with pea-green handles forged in the shape of a naked woman; old golf balls indented with canine tooth marks; a plastic pipette with a squeezy red rubber balloon on the end; silver doilies, a hairnet, a soap with a rose transfer, a cork with a man's head on it which, when you pulled the lever, moved his jaw. Endless grit and dirt and fluff. Stray pieces of Winalot and a flea collar from when she had a dog. And a packet of pins.

I still don't understand how the pins turned up that day.

'Now then,' she said, one wet, winter afternoon, coming in and placing a plate on the tapestry pouffe, 'I've done you some flapjacks.'

We were doing pictures with felt tips, our cheeks flushed by the electric fire, the window a sheet of colourless water. There was a musical on TV in black and white, with the sound turned down. Granny often watched without sound. She'd seen a silent version of *The Sound of Music* four times.

Sara put the lid on her pen and took a biscuit. Penny and I scrambled to do the same, spilling pens down the cracks in the sofa in our hurry.

It was hard, at first, to understand why a piece of flapjack should be prickly and painful. I didn't move, couldn't swallow. Penny gave a little cry and spat hers out all over her lap. Sara had not yet bitten. I put my hankie up to my mouth and emptied the mess of prickle and sweetness out.

'What is it?' Granny asked. But her arms were folded and she had her feet up. She seemed abnormally relaxed, almost smiling.

'Pins,' said Penny, and her face got ready to cry.

'Sorry,' I said, 'but I think there are pins in them, Granny.'

But she looked calm.

'Oh dear. Oh dear, well, spit them out.' She stared at

me and with a fingernail she tested a tiny ladder in her stocking.

Penny began to cry.

Humming to herself, Granny cleared the plates away and then I heard her washing up, the kitchen tap running.

'She's old,' I told my sisters, with a niggling sense of loss. 'Going mad, isn't she?' and we carried on with our drawings, but it wasn't the same.

I carry Jack up to the loft in his basket – negotiating the ladder whilst clutching the straw handles – and sit very still holding my paints. I stare for a long time at all my canvases, stacked against the wall, most of them half-finished. Nothing, I now realize, to do with me. I watch over them like dead friends, wait for them to speak to me, convey something wordless and worthwhile, but of course they don't.

The separate images now strike me as crude and naïve, straightforward like the guileless, blameless paintings of a child. Even my new one, my favourite, started in that long ago dim hinterland just days before Jack's birth – with the bold layers of pink and honey and violet like a bruise, the scarlet which threatened to take control – I now realize is nothing. Just random blocks of colour – phoney, useless. So what? Oh well, I think, I can't paint this – this hurtling towards death, oblivion. Out of the window, I fix my eyes upon the white, unmoving, unchanging sky.

Then Jack begins to cry and I sit down to feed him, releasing the clip on my bra — grateful for the necessary calm.

The day after my call to Lenny, I find him on my doorstep. I suppose I should have realized he'd do that, but my sense of withdrawal is so complete now, so finished and perfected, that I don't have a vision of the rest of the world moving out there. It seems to me we're all just glued into our separate spaces, aloof and morose, with our separate babies and our separate ghosts.

He sits on the sofa. I am opposite, my hands folded in my lap, on the cane chair. I wear an old plaid shirt of Alistair's, leggings, no make up. Something is simmering on the hob in the kitchen and I'm slightly perturbed that I can't remember what it is — cabbage, carrot, cod? Jack lies on a mat and gazes at a coat-hanger which I strung with brightly coloured stars and balls before his birth when I was bright and happy.

'A neat house,' says Lenny, looking round. Then he puts his head in his hands and cries.

Queenie had not intended to be with him at the end. The nurses did ask, but she declined the offer and went back to her room to shuffle cards and wait. She sharpened her bridge pencils. She wrote a letter to a friend in Canada asking if she might come and stay in a month or two. She thought about redecorating the bungalow at Normanton-on-Soar, maybe laying a parquet floor in the drawing-room. Pearl had one and it was very smart. It was almost midnight.

At about 12.10 a.m., she went to the bathroom to prepare for bed and, passing the room, decided to put her head around the door and ask the nurse to let her know when it was all over. But the moment she stepped inside, she realized there was a terrible noise coming from the bed – a kind of rattling, choking sound.

'Oh, Mrs Hancock,' said the nurse, looking slightly pink but otherwise doggedly tranquil, 'this is it, I'm afraid. He's just going.'

Transfixed, still as a rabbit hypnotized by headlamps, Queenie stared at the head on the pillow. She had no choice, her body forced her to watch. His eyes were just open and his face was a dark shade of plum and it was his breath that was rattling so horribly. It took no more than a few seconds. Almost before the noise had really stopped, the nurse quickly used her fingers to close his eyes and drew a little breath and glanced at her, a meaningless glance, devoid of fear or pain.

Queenie tightened her lips and folded her arms, stroking the soft nap of her sleeve with her fingers. 'Is that it, then?' She was free. Free to go. She ought to be pleased and, in a sense, she was. But it was truly irritating to have been there with him at the end after all, even accidentally.

*

'Do you love him?' Lenny asks me, again. 'Do you really love Alistair? Because if the answer is yes, then I'll try and leave you alone — I mean it, I will.' He looks down at a battered leather wallet which he rolls and unrolls in his fingers — long pale fingers which have touched me more memorably than any fingers ever.

'I can't lie and cheat any more,' I say. 'It's all this having to lie. I just can't do it — I have a little baby, Lenny . . . you know that.'

'You haven't answered my question,' he says, glancing up, and the space under his eyes is pink with unshed tears. That pink space is painful to me.

'Look,' I say, coldly, getting up, getting desperate, 'look, I'll phone you. I'll phone you this week, before the end of the week, OK? I promise, if you'll go now.'

I say it to get rid of him, to get him away, out of my house, because I've begun to feel so very jeopardized.

Another moment and I might have blown it. I might have thrown my arms around his neck and wept.

The day after the funeral, Queenie gathered together everything she could find that had been his and was not valuable enough to sell and burnt it. She made a bonfire at the bottom of the garden, beyond the gazebo, where the gardener burned the rotten leaves and dead branches every year.

It was a Saturday afternoon, and neither Deirdre nor

Bonny, the daily maid, were in the house, so she got Douglas to help her carry the piles of clothes and shoes and papers down the path. Even the oil paintings he'd done before their marriage – horses and some very ordinary sunsets. They worked in silence, trudging backwards and forwards, the smoke catching at the backs of their throats, filling their hair each time the wind changed. Twigs snapped constantly underfoot.

Bonny had cleaned his room as soon as the body had been removed by the undertakers, but it still smelt of perspiration, whisky (which he'd needed in vast quantities right up until the end) and of the unmistakable sour sweetness of death. Now, as Queenie stood at the bottom of the garden stoking the fire, she could see the window was still flung wide and the curtains flew like flags, silent, congratulatory reminders that she was free. As soon as the smell had gone, she thought she might use it as a second dressing-room, for spare shoes and hats and so on.

All afternoon the bonfire raged. The last things she brought from the house were his family photographs – Josiah and Evelina Hancock on their wedding day, George and his brother Horace on a rug with teething rings, George at sixteen in his first suit, George in leather helmet on a motorbike. These she dropped into the scorching centre of the fire with a final flourish – pale faces existing for one last second before they withered for ever, drowning in a sea of flame. Douglas was silent throughout, but as she turned for the last time towards the house, she glanced at the back of him and noticed a wide dark stain spreading over the seat of his trousers. He was blubbing silently.

'Ugh,' she exclaimed with genuine distaste, because Deirdre was off and she was going to have to deal with it herself, 'you're six years old, Douglas, and you've wet your pants. You're disgusting.'

On the mahogany table in Granny's hall there was a photo of Daddy as a teenager on horseback in Skegness, another of her standing next to a sports car, her fingers lightly resting on the gleaming bonnet, and at least two or three photos of various dogs she'd had – Sabre, a diabetic pitbull terrier, and Gretchen, the dachshund.

'Oh, we didn't get on,' she conceded, when we asked about our grandfather and why there were no pictures of him. 'He was a terrible drinker – all the photos were destroyed in a fire . . .' she added, putting her legs, with their knots and brown spots and varicose veins, on a pouffe. 'Douglas doesn't remember . . .'

Our father came and sat down at this point, working a cigarette up out of a packet with one hand, whilst reaching for Granny's heavy silver lighter with the other. He looked at her and lit the cigarette in silence, and we sensed, then, an awful moment. But Granny went on sipping her drink and looked steadily at him, and the moment hung in the air like the taste of smoke, before passing away almost without trace.

*

sleepwalking

Jack has started to cry a lot in the evenings. When he's not feeding, he has to be walked up and down on someone's shoulder. Then he'll calm down, but won't sleep, and looks around instead with beady, fretful eyes. As soon as you try to sit down, or even lean against something, he cries again — long, bitter cries, as if betrayed in some unspeakable way. We're both exhausted with it.

Because I haven't managed to cook us any supper, Alistair fetches a take-away, and a video. We get as far as the opening shots and Jack starts up again. 'Here, I'll take him,' he says with forced patience, fork in hand. I pass him over and sit back on the sofa with a sigh, resting my head, too tired to eat.

Al puts him firmly in his pram and turns up the sound on the TV as Jack draws breath for the first wail. I go into the kitchen to fetch a glass of water. The house is filled with the mixed crescendo of the video and our baby's voice. But nothing stops this one, this other child. He's waiting there in the kitchen, leaning against the wall beneath the spice rack, watching my face with undisguised hatred.

'What do you want?' I ask, as quietly as I can, surprised all the same to hear my small scared voice. 'What is it? What do you want?'

He smiles, he extends the palm of his thin and wretched hand, and there's time for me to see it quite clearly — to note the slightly scabby red lines where there's a dreadful rash, like eczema. Then he's fading away, the line and colour of his form becoming one with the wall.

'Jesus! Oh Christ!' I've had enough, I raise my hands and smack them down against the edges of the space, where I can still see the cowlick of his hair, the miserable slope of his skinny shoulder. I want to damage him before he goes, to stop him fading, bring him back, slap him into the real world and make him account for himself. But he's gone and the weight of my hand crashes down hard on to the spice rack and Alistair races into the room with Jack on his shoulder, to find me, flushed and angry in a cloud of paprika and ground cloves, blood on my hands, and the broken fragments of the jars around my feet.

'Bloody hell, Susan,' he says. We stand, staring at one another. For the first time in hours, Jack is quiet.

When Douglas told his mother he was going to marry Barbara, she had to go to bed for a week.

'I'm thirty-seven next birthday, Mother,' he said, and tried to scare her with the hatred in his eyes. 'Why don't I bring her home to tea?' Queenie grudgingly dressed and got in some pastries, but she didn't bother with best china or anything, and when the girl arrived, she made a point of sending her back into the hall to wipe her feet.

'I'm sorry,' she said, with outstretched arms, enjoying the silvery kiss of her bracelets against the silky underneath of her wrist, 'only the cleaner's just been, and I wouldn't want to have to Hoover it again myself. There's only Douglas and me, you know.'

For he was her mate, her companion; she leaned on him in every way except physically. Physically, she never touched him – never had, even as a boy. But still she knew she got a vague thrill, as she watched him slip his jacket off, put it over the back of a chair, lay his wallet on the hall table. There was no substitute for living with a man, rather than the drunken spaniel that George had been. Queenie was sixty-three years old. She looked at the young girl. She looked at those long limbs and smooth brown hair and wide brown eyes and felt a sort of fury, as though someone had directly criticized her. She looked at her good teeth and her small breasts and creamy skin and wondered how she could hurt her. 'We're going to be good friends, I'm sure,' she said, placing a wrinkled, bejewelled hand on the girl's perfect knee. Barbara's mother was a foreigner and her father was a failure. They lived in a mobile home with an outside lavatory, near Colwick.

'Well, I can see what she sees in you,' she told Douglas, later, 'I just hope you're not being taken for a ride, that's all. I should think her parents are preening themselves.' She was pleased, anyway, when Douglas agreed that after the wedding – which was set for August – they'd live with her while they took their time and looked for a house. And even then it was settled that they wouldn't live more than a mile away.

'He'll be back,' she told herself later, as she caught the last ten minutes of *Miss World* on TV, 'before you can say Jack Robinson . . .'

*

Jack and I go to see Ede at the gallery.

It's pouring with rain – long straight grey lines dancing off the wide pavements – and we park on a meter in the next street and race along under my half-broken umbrella, Jack jogging peacefully against my breast in the sling. Buses and lorries send fans of black water up into the gutters. The gallery's busier than usual, full of people waiting for the rain to stop. Lenny's exhibition came down more than a week ago and there are now some minimally framed black and white photographs on the wall – large emphatically ugly portraits of skinny waitresses and models, transvestites in Paris and prostitutes at King's Cross.

'Ha! It's called "Female Metropolis",' Ede tells me, waving a wad of press releases. 'We're only doing it for the money,' of course – they sell extremely well, you'd be amazed. So, how's my favourite little boy?' She plants a cigarette-scented kiss on Jack's head, but he continues to sleep. We go into the office at the back and she pours me coffee. Several paintings are stacked against the wall, wrapped in bubble-pack. I know without being told that they are Lenny's.

'OK,' says Ede, swathing her small tense form in her large oatmeal cardigan, 'OK, are you ready for the big news?' She takes a breath. 'I'm getting married.' She fidgets with her rings, glancing up at me with a serious and sheepish face, but her excitement is barely contained. It's appalling but, for one terrible moment, I think it's Lenny. It's something to do with his pictures sitting there, stacked against the wall. So my response is not quite right. I flush, I panic: 'What?' I say, quickly. 'Oh Ede, who?' But she doesn't notice. She roots in her bag for a cigarette.

'Well,' she says, 'you don't know him. Julian – he's an actor, though strangely enough we met when he tried to sell me advertising. That's what he does when he's not working. A cold call!' She rolls her eyes. On her temple, I can see the blue veins through the thin veil of skin. Full of hope – of chances, I think.

'But when . . .?' I am relieved. So relieved I'm ashamed.

'Oh Suze, don't say it's too soon. When you know, you just know. It feels completely right. What can I do? He asked me and I just couldn't have said no.' And now there are tears in her eyes. 'I've been lonely, you know.' Strangely, I've never ever thought this, not of Ede. She carries people along with her, always talking, arranging. Outside, the rain has almost stopped and the sky is clearing. Beads of light gather on the fire escape outside the office window. 'I thought we'd wait till spring – April or May, I can't stand winter. It won't be a big thing,' she continues, 'we just want our closest friends . . . and you know, I was thinking, would you feel OK about Alistair and Lenny both being there? Because there's no way round it really, is there?'

'It's wonderful, I'm so pleased,' I say, as we hug, with Jack between us.

'Oh Susan, Susan,' says Ede, stroking the imperceptible little line on Jack's forehead where his soft black hair peters into the down of his cheek, 'I can't bear it – you look so sad.'

*

Julie Myerson

Granny didn't understand about children.

The Christmas I was nine, I made her a pair of slippers. I found a pattern in my mother's *Golden Hands* magazine and made a cardboard template from a cereal packet. We bought green felt from Jessop's.

I cut them out and stitched them in blanket stitch, taking care to make the stitches even in length.

'Very good,' said Mummy, when I held them up, 'very good, very neat.'

In the spare room sewing chest we found some boxes of sequins and beads — tiny pink dots like coloured rice and sparkly blue ones. You had to sew each bead on individually, which took ages, but was worth it because when I'd finished the slippers were perfect — the toes of each one spangled with its own pattern, a metallic milky way. I wrapped them in tissue paper and put them in a shoe box. Sara said they were so good they looked bought.

But on Christmas Day, Granny hardly looked at them. 'Oh,' she said, 'I'm afraid they're too big, much too big — I've always had tiny feet, you know,' and she was right because she held up a stockinged foot and the slipper was way too big — a good inch and a half longer. 'You'd be best keeping them for someone else,' she said, handing them back in their tissue paper, never even having taken them right out. 'Someone with bigger feet. Haven't you got big feet, Barbara?'

Our mother lit a cigarette. She didn't answer for a moment. I waited.

'She made them herself, Queenie,' she inhaled and flicked a crumb off her sleeve, 'for God's sake.'

Yes, I thought, I did – swallowing.

'Oh, did she?' Granny looked not at me but at Mummy, her jaw lengthening as she feigned surprise. 'All the more reason then, not to waste them. I'd be slopping around all over the place in them. I mean, they'd be dangerous.'

I didn't speak to Granny for the rest of that day, but I don't know whether she noticed.

Later, we watched *Little Women* on TV and I cried my heart out when Beth died.

Lenny does not know it, but I am in a photocopying shop on his street watching his front door. Jack is in the buggy, fast asleep under a tartan blanket with his rainhood up, and in front of me someone is complaining because the copies they've made have come out too dark. It is 10.30 a.m. A sunless February morning, sky like charcoal dust.

I know Lenny will come out soon.

I don't know why I need to do this, to spy. I have to see how he is without me. Maybe there will be a clue – in his face, in his clothes, in the way he shuts the door or glances down the street – that will prove to me I've done the right thing.

Because we're a family, now – Alistair and Susan and Jack. There's no going back. I did the right thing. Next Christmas, we'll send cards with those names on, written in joyful, looped writing, with three kisses underneath — Alistair, Susan and Jack. Jack will be a whole year old, and maybe pulling himself to stand at our glass-topped coffee table. Alistair will photograph his first drunken steps. He'll have top and bottom teeth. He'll have his milk out of a cup. But for now, I stand here in this photocopying shop, because I have to see what I'm missing — that I'm missed. 'Excuse me,' says a woman by the machine, 'are you waiting?'

'No,' I reply, pushing the buggy away from the queue and closer to the window, 'No, go ahead . . .'

'I'm not giving you three fifty for those,' continues the man who is still complaining, 'absolutely bloody useless they are to me, now.'

'Never happy, are they?' smiles the woman who's now using the machine. She collects the papers up with an expression of complete serenity. 'Love your baby,' she adds, as she goes to pay.

I glance at Jack and then out of the window. A thin drizzle of rain has started. The black door is opening. Lenny comes quickly down the steps, head down, wrapping a scarf around his neck. I tense and flush, watching him, willing him to lift his face, so that I can judge from his expression whether he still loves me or not.

After an hour of crying, Jack has at last gone to sleep in his crib by the bed.

'Hold me,' says Alistair, softly but insistent, pressing his erection against my thigh. Oh God, I think, recognizing some sort of a test. It's not his fault. I used to do this. I used to love him. We cannot make love – it's not quite six weeks and I'm still sore – but there's nothing to stop me doing this now. If I love him.

'Come here,' I say, and I fold my body against his. My husband. He smells of soap, of garlic, and a little of sweat. I press my mouth against his face and think of kissing, examining the area around his mouth with my lips. He encourages his prick into my hand.

'Ah,' he says, and lets out a little sigh, then a moan.

'I love you,' I say, mesmerized by the slow, slanting shadows of passing car headlights moving across the ceiling, and finishing the job as quickly as I can.

Queenie was quite disgusted when, only a month after they got back from the honeymoon, Douglas told her Barbara was pregnant.

'Due in May,' he said, adding unnecessarily, 'You'll be a grandmother.' Rubbing it in.

'Well, you didn't waste any time, did you?' was her reply, as she trimmed the rind off a piece of bacon. 'Here,' she said, handing the thread of yellow fat to him, 'hang this on the birdhouse for the tits.'

She was still the one he turned to, anyway, she made sure of that. Every morning she was up and dressed first –

bathed, creamed, powdered, perfumed. She'd make herself a pot of tea and sit in the kitchen reading yesterday's *Evening Post*, starting with the obituaries. She was only in her sixties and already acquaintances were dropping like flies. By the time Douglas and Barbara came down – he'd usually get to Josiah Hancock Ltd., where he was now Managing Director, by about nine – she'd got on to yesterday's TV page and her second cup of tea.

Barbara's presence in her house irritated her from the start, but as her pregnancy advanced, she began to find the mere sight of her – the shameless emblem, the proof, of her son's sexuality – infinitely more offensive.

'Can't you cover yourself?' she snapped, as the girl got up in her dressing-gown to cook his breakfast, the distended stomach quite evident through the nylon garment. 'You really do look a sight, you know.'

One afternoon she came back from shopping to find her sitting right in the middle of her immaculate biscuit-coloured sofa, crying. Queenie put down her carrier bags and stood in the doorway for a moment, watching.

'Whatever is it?'

'I want to go home, I'm not happy, if you must know,' said Barbara, between sobs, 'but I haven't even got the bloody bus fare.' She glanced up at Queenie as if she did not care any more what she said. Her mascara had run down her face, till the grey streaks were almost level with her nose. She looked absurd, clownish, spoiled – not pretty at all.

'Well, for Heaven's sake,' said Queenie, in a low, artificially kind voice. She forced a smile. 'Here, you'll be doing my son a favour, I'm sure.' The coin didn't quite fall flat, but rocked for a moment on the coffee table as the two women stared at one another.

But when Douglas came home he took Barbara out for dinner all lovey-dovey and, when Queenie went downstairs to watch TV, the coin was still there on the table, a large, accusing eye winking fiercely back at her.

six

'The individual is actually awake, but in another world.'

I try to stay mostly in the kitchen because that's where he's least likely to come. It's nearly always the bedroom, or the landing – he's often waiting after I've changed Jack's nappy, slouching in the shadows against the bookcase and the ferns, empty eyed, staring past me. I turn away, I pretend not to see, I tell myself I'm wrong. Firmly, I pull a shutter down over my own ridiculous imaginings, my self-imposed haunting. I seriously wonder whether I should seek some sort of help – counselling, anything.

'Marriage guidance!' Alistair snorts, on the verge of anger. 'What on earth are you trying to tell me?'

'Al,' I say, more meekly than I intended, 'it's not personal. It's not you – this is me.'

'Oh yes,' he replies, in a bitter voice I've never heard him use, 'oh, yes, you. Everything comes back to you, doesn't it, eventually.' He does not look at me. I watch the side of his face as he pours himself a beer. There's no expression – only the look of someone pouring a beer. I balance Jack on my knees after his feed, gently rubbing his back. A huge burp comes up, bringing with it a quantity of undigested milk all over my jeans.

'A cloth please, Alistair, quick . . .'

He hands me a piece of kitchen towel, glancing down absently at Jack as he does so. Then, more gently and with surprising perspicacity, 'Is this about sex, Susan? Is that it?'

'You're depressed, aren't you?' On the phone, Ede comes straight out with it. 'This is plain and simple post-natal depression, and if Alistair can't see it, then I'm bloody well going to have to talk to him . . .'

In a corner of the sitting-room, just, almost, out of the field of my vision, he stalks me, his thin arms outstretched, like a sleepwalker.

I should have known, really. It was always going to be impossible to keep Lenny away.

He catches me up in The Chase – he must have been waiting for me, knowing I might take that route to the Common. I push Jack briskly, the buggy wheels squeaking in the dirt. Another day, squat and cold, the sky greyer and lower by the minute, an airtight lid on the world. He touches me on the shoulder. I stop and we stand under the skeleton of an ash tree, litter and leaves blowing around our feet. He thrusts his hands down in his pockets, tilts his head, and I tremble.

'Come back with me now.'

I'm silent. I've even forgotten how to speak to him. My

nose is running in the cold and the wind. I grope in my pockets for a tissue. Jack cries because the buggy's stopped. He looks at me steadily, then takes my face in both his hands and kisses me, so hungry, so sad. I see in close-up the coarse black fabric of his coat, the pale hair against his collar, the long fingers, nails ingrained with blue and grey paint.

I hold his fingers. 'What've you been painting?' I push my face against his sleeve.

We walk back to his car which is parked on the next road, and I sit in the back with Jack on my knee and the belt over both of us, because there's no baby seat.

At six forty-five in the evening, Douglas ran Barbara to the hospital – she was already doubled over with the pains. But once they got there, everything stopped and Barbara, perspiring and guilty, said, 'You go home. They'll call you if anything happens.'

So he drove back. It was a delicate hot May evening, the trees loaded with blossom, the birds singing. They were still living with his mother, having decided to look for a house after the baby was born. She'd put a lamb chop on for his supper. At nine o'clock, Queenie glanced at her watch.

'I had you in about forty-five minutes flat, you know,' she remarked. 'I didn't hang about – you were out just like that . . .'

sleepwalking

At ten o'clock, they drank some Scotch on the patio together. 'I wouldn't bother ringing,' said Queenie, 'she's probably asleep now.' At eleven o'clock, the air still blowing warm and fragrant through the bathroom window, they went to bed. At seven the next morning, the hospital rang. Douglas stumbled out of bed to answer it, ragged faced in his open pyjama top and Y-fronts.

'Well?' Queenie appeared at the top of the stairs as he replaced the receiver.

'A girl,' he said, 'a girl, ten minutes ago.'

'Ah well,' said Queenie, 'better luck next time . . .'

I had blue eyes and fair hair and a huge claret-coloured birthmark all over my bottom which my parents were reassured would fade in time. Daddy wanted to call me Diana after Diana Dors, and Mummy wanted me to be Elizabeth, after the Queen. In the end they just called me Susan.

Daddy balanced me on his knee as he watched television, one arm supporting my back, the other holding his cigarette.

'She's a real Daddy's girl,' he smiled. I made no noise, just smiled back at him and waved my arms, and when he'd had enough he put me down.

Lenny opens me up again, easy as pressing his thumb down

on a milk bottle top. I am cold and complete and he opens me – licks me, stirs me, laps me up.

This time there's no particular gentleness, no reticence, neither of us stints: we are deprived people in a deprived landscape – we have to do it, grab what we can. Jack is good, angelic even: he sleeps, and then when he wakes, for the first time ever he just lies there without crying on the folded blanket waiting for us to finish. As if he can sense the hard crackle in the air – the caught breath, the pulling and pushing, the thing which can't be hurried, must end in its own time.

He must never know, of course. He'll never know that his mother took her lover in his presence in that unironed bed in front of the gas fire. When I come, Lenny presses hard fingers over my mouth, but the cry is ragged and needy, half-hearted almost. I'm neither ashamed nor disloyal this time. My need is a childish thing, and I fulfil it without thinking, like a child.

I'm still here, I notice afterwards, amazed, and this time I don't question anything, I just breathe and wait for my heartbeat to subside. Afterwards, I take Jack into the bed to give him what milk hasn't leaked over Lenny and into the sheets, and we all three fall asleep again together. I wake an hour later to see the two heads – one pale, one dark – on the crumpled sheets, and my heart almost bursts with the pain.

Outside it's icy – a sharp petrified city. By three o'clock, a black line seems to have formed around the sun.

sleepwalking

'Tell me the truth,' I say to Lenny, 'do you really believe in ghosts?' He pulls the coffee-stained duvet up to our necks and peels us a tangerine. He looks at me and doesn't laugh.

The long grass in Daddy's orchard was littered with apples all going to waste. Wasps climbed in and out of the brown holes, clinging to the flesh. At six o'clock, as he watched *Sale of the Century* on TV, I collected some whole ones up and put them in a bag by the front door to take home for cooking. But at seven, when Ray's brown Ford car drew up outside, the bag was gone, simply removed. He never said a word to me about it.

'Goodbye, Susan,' he said, turning his face away, and balanced his cigarette carefully on the edge of the ashtray, before kissing Penny and Sara's upturned mouths.

That was the last time I ever saw him.

When he wrote the following week, he said that he found me impudent and disloyal and that his psychiatrist had advised him that it would be less painful and disruptive for him if he stopped seeing me for the time being. I was fifteen.

'Funny,' said Mummy, 'I had no idea he was under a psychiatrist.' I cried that night in bed, but fell asleep very quickly, and slept a cool sleep of relief.

A month later, he was all but gone from my mind and everything looked brighter. I no longer dreaded every other weekend. It was as if he'd died – conveniently and painlessly – and all that remained of him was this bad dream I had now and then. I always forgot the dream very quickly, and attached no particular significance to it. In fact, when I first met Alistair and he asked me about my father, I answered without a moment's thought that he was dead and was shocked to remember, seconds later, that this was in fact completely untrue.

'Do you know,' I tell Alistair, suddenly, 'my father never loved me – in fact I know now that he hated me, he blamed me. You'll never do that, will you – you'll never blame Jack – if things don't work out for you, if you become disenchanted . . .?' If I leave you, I think.

We sit on the sofa drinking red wine, eating cashews. Alistair laughs, puts an arm around my waist, squeezes at the flesh which is still soft and loose, where it stretched itself to contain Jack.

'Poor old girl,' he says, reaching past me to put on the TV for the news, 'how're we going to cheer you up? I think what we probably need is a romantic weekend away.'

I lie on top of Lenny without moving, the repetition of his heart deep in my belly. My thighs are open, wet, warm. The clock ticks. It's obvious that we're stuck. We've both baled out and now there's only sex.

sleepwalking

'I ought to go,' I say. He touches my neck with his tongue, but doesn't bother to argue.

It wouldn't be true to say I'm ready for him this time, but the only real shock is that he goes straight to Jack — ignoring me and making his way to my baby. That I'm not prepared for, and won't tolerate.

There are of course little warning signs, slight enough things I can now pick up: there's an oppressive thickness, a pulsing tightness in the air, an almost familiar buzz which catches at the back of my throat. When I open my eyes that morning, I am already tense, my head straining on the pillow. I know he'll come, and that it will be different somehow.

So. I say goodbye to Alistair, incline my head for his kiss. Despite the light sprinkle of rain, a blackbird is singing, loud and discordant, by the back door. At ten o'clock I pile the breakfast dishes in the sink, put Jack down for his sleep, plug in the baby alarm, and by ten past I'm in the loft. It's so dark, I have to put all the lights on. I stand for a moment gazing at the door, a vague, cold sense of something unidentifiable that I ought to do, raging through me. It's a wet, windy morning, and through the skylight above my head the clouds are scudding, fast and mad. I sit with my colours and palettes and canvas, and know I cannot work. Ten more minutes pass. And then I hear it.

'Ickle baby . . .' A child's voice – secretive, petulant, nasal – crackling over the baby alarm. Then, 'Twinkle, twinkle silly brat . . .' A grown man, slurring his words, muffled with alcohol. Unmistakable. In Jack's room. In his room.

I don't wait to work it out, for the realization to sink in. I don't wait for the terror to drag its jagged length along my spine, I don't know about the stairs or remember how I jump over the washing basket, round the corner and fling open his half-shut door. I only experience my own shout, a suffering sound which comes from my lungs, some-where behind my eyes, a sound I've never heard before – monstrous, penetrating the air in a live and dangerous way, like gelignite – exploding against the familiar silence of that room: bears and rabbits, cotton-wool pleats and blankets. Though the Noah's Ark blinds are drawn, any sense of real darkness comes only from the terrible shadowy form beside my baby's cot.

'Get out! Get the fuck out!' Once I've started, it's imposs-ible to stop. 'Get out! Get out!' I continue to shout – fear preventing any hiatus. Then a whoosh of expletives. Twenty years of fury fighting themselves free of me in one terrified scream.

He does not move. He looks straight at me, his eyes two small shocks of yellow light – empty, purposeless, dead. Then he smiles, and that mouth begins to work. Man's voice pours out – vomits, spits, swoops around the room on wings, violent and unexpected. The air reeks of whisky.

And Jack? Jack is smiling up at his grandfather, reaching out with small fists, joyfully kicking the blankets off his feet, waiting to be picked up.

I know what's going to happen next, but before he can reach his skinny arms down towards my baby, I'm there — in one quick movement, snatching Jack against me, moving to the door. I cry out once more as I feel his foul breath on my face, his fingers scrabbling at my clothes, at the ragged bottom of my painting sweater.

'Oh,' he says, 'oh!' crying with his child's fury. I push at the air and someone laughs, a cold stab of a laugh, catching at the base of my spine.

I clutch my baby and scream.

'No, Daddy, no!'

Terror and disgust turn to a trembling relief as the upright position causes Jack to burp, and I'm aware that the room is suddenly still, and there's only an angry flare of light in the spot up till then inhabited by his wicked, wicked face.

We sit on the front doorstep in the gloomy late morning, me and Jack, because frankly nowhere else seems very safe. He sucks warm microwaved milk happily from his bottle. We watch the pavement where ragged birds peck at litter and listen to the safe sound, down the street, of a Peter Jones delivery van.

The second post comes — some bills, circulars, something

189

from a book club for Alistair, and the postman hands them to me with amused surprise. He thinks we must be locked out. I try not to shiver.

We sit there for a long time.

Alistair and I have our weekend in the country in March.

He arranges it, books the hotel – a pale stone mansion in the lush green and grey countryside outside Bath: turquoise chintz bedrooms, wide, uneven stairs, corridors hazy with breakfast smells and perfume. It rains all the first day. Every time we think of going for a walk it pours again, so we sit for hours drinking weak coffee on a window seat overlooking the perfect wet sloping lawns.

We try to relax – well, we pretend. Alistair flicks through the weekend section of *The Times* in the last dregs of afternoon light, now and then laughing and reading something out to me. He makes a point of including me, his hand resting sometimes on my knee, sometimes brushing my shoulder. I bite my nails and attempt to feed Jack under my jumper. It's so dark that a man comes in and – with apologies and some fuss – turns on the heavy, old-fashioned standard lamp. When he leaves the room the bulb dims, flickers, and finally goes out again. We laugh half-heartedly, grateful for the dull mask of dusk.

We go up and change slowly and meticulously for dinner while Jack lies kicking on the lumpy king-size bed. In the bathroom, Alistair tries to kiss me, but the hot tap's running, steaming up the mirror, and then we hear Jack being a bit sick. We deal with that, and then when I come back in wrapped in a towel, Alistair's sitting in just his shirt and underpants, zapping through the channels on the TV.

'Come here,' he says, holding out a hand but not turning round.

I pick the baby up and go and sit beside him. The motor racing's on – dust and droning, cloud and metal. Jack's eyes widen and a milky bubble appears between his lips.

'Look,' I say, 'look at his face – he's so alert. He's actually watching it.'

Alistair laughs and strokes the dark little head and turns off the TV and then we all three just lie on the bed for a while, very close and still, a pocket of silence holding us together. Outside, wind in the trees, cars on the gravel, loud male voices. Jack's fingers brush the towel, flutter round my breasts. My limbs cave in, I almost go to sleep.

Minutes pass, and then Alistair reaches across and touches me. His hand is surprisingly remote and small. Something in the way his fingers move – gentle and guarded – says that he knows this might not be it, that I'm not necessarily his. Despite everything, I'm shocked at his hesitation, find it awful and sad. I caress his hand and he takes a quick breath and I find myself moving my thighs apart for him – as if they were someone else's. Close by I smell Jack's warm swirl of hair and a trace of vomit.

'Oh,' Alistair's sighing now, his breath in my ear, 'oh Susan . . .'

Jack has worked my towel down and is searching for a nipple, small butterfly hands moving, and I feel the pricking of the milk, the warm shock of his mouth. And in that particular instant I think, something's changed, something's making sense. But it has nothing to do with either of them, what they're doing. It's not that. No, it's me – it's that I'm moving somehow, moving on, seeing things differently.

Far away down the corridor, a door slams and there's laughter, but it's as nothing to me because I'm already moving away – out and away – from this bed, this hotel, this whole warm place. A part of me is drifting, floating. I almost see my own body down there on the bed, limbs spread, feeding my child, opening to my husband.

'Put him in the cot,' Alistair says, his hand dipping down between my buttocks, pulling me closer, but I kiss his hand, reach for the light, careful not to disengage Jack.

'Look, he's feeding again already and I'm starving. Let's eat first.'

And there I am, I've come back. Woken from a long sleep. Pulled back. They don't seem surprised to see me at all.

Five minutes later Alistair watches me dress.

I ruffle my hair, put on lipstick, feel the cool fabric of my dress slip over my head. I notice, with a touch of suspicion, that my mood is too perfect, trance-like. I dress deliberately, for him. I think about how we'll make love later – how he'll strip me and press his body along mine, a seamless joining of torsos, and I'll be just drunk and tired enough. Because this is what we came here for.

And me, where am I in all this? Who has made me like it? What is it I know now that I didn't know before?

Well, I don't think I want Lenny but, glancing at the bedside table, I realize I still can't see a telephone without his number thumping its live, sore beat through my solar plexus.

We plug Jack into a special listening device so the receptionist can alert us if he cries. On the way to the dining-room, Alistair puts an arm around my shoulders. I try to appreciate this.

'Like old times,' he laughs, ten minutes later, shaking out his napkin and raising his glass. 'Well, almost.'

When they bring the pudding trolley round, he chooses, after much deliberation and questioning of the waiter, something chocolate. Afterwards, we drink liqueurs in a large room with an open fire. Alistair looks me in the eyes without shame.

'Susan,' he says, 'come on.'

We do it in the dark, quietly. We sweat a lot. We don't speak at all. Jack's breath pierces the intense silence. In a way, I admit it, I do want it, want him; in a way, I don't. Afterwards, Alistair reaches over to put on the light, pours a glass of water.

'Are you happy?' he asks, squinting in the brightness. He is still lying on top of me, his prick worming out as it relaxes. His voice is clear, sober.

'Why?'

'Well, I wondered.' He shifts his weight off me, props his head on his elbow, 'This evening was — well, it is — going so well. But I never know with you. I just wondered.'

I flush, turn my face to the wall, pretending to check Jack. Some demon pushes me toward an unperceived edge. But why? Why now?

'I've been having an affair,' I say, quietly, but loud enough. Semen trickles down the inside of my thigh. 'But it's over.'

Well, I think. Well. My belly is tense. Look, I think — look, I've told the truth.

He is quiet. I wait. Then he laughs.

'You're joking.' I am silent. 'You're joking? You're teasing me?' He kisses my shoulder, he sounds convinced, 'Tell me you're joking — you're a funny girl.'

'I'm joking,' I say — because he sounds so convinced.

He gets up and goes to the bathroom. The bang of the lid. A heavy stream of piss.

'If you've been having an affair with anyone,' he says, coming back in, 'it's been with that baby. It's not your fault. We should have done something like this before. We've had no time together. I feel I've got you back at last.'

He pulls me to him, folds my head against his shoulder. I close my eyes, listening to the baby sucking his fingers in his sleep, to the wind and the rain.

Part of me is sucked out. The idea of falling comes into my head. Bodies falling from tall buildings, from sky-scraping trees, out of the skies. I'm high up, looking down on that windswept field again, that man. The pitch black, the lurch of gravity. I shut my eyes. I'd like to be comforted, but there's no one who can do it.

'Why did you say that?' he asks me, then, 'About having an affair? It was an odd thing to say. What good could it do?'

'What good can anything do?' I reply, brittle and ungiving as ice.

When he's asleep I wriggle off him.

I can't sleep, but I'm so calm. I shake out a couple of paracetamol, and swallow them with a glass of mineral water.

At six thirty the next morning, after I've fed Jack, with Alistair still snoring gently on his side of the bed, I dress quickly, pulling on my leggings, jumper and jacket, not bothering with underwear or to brush my hair, and creep off down the corridor. I hear the squeak of a trolley in the dining-room, the multiple chink of glasses, low female voices, the smell of early morning tea, but I hurry past guiltily and out of the huge front door, which looks as if it should be locked, but isn't.

It's a perfect morning, misty and cold, barely light – the sky whitening as darkness pours off it. I'm alert, quite alone, in the countryside. I run down the gravel drive, on to the wet lawns, and beyond over a stile into the fields.

My plimsolls and leggings are soaked — sun struggles to break through the colourless trees. Some strange water bird calls, more a shout, a wail. Otherwise, only the hiss of pylons whose heads disappear in the mist — and the twitter of nameless first birds. I don't feel like a mother any more, nor anyone's wife or lover. I don't feel like anyone. I've been waiting to do this since I don't know when. I'm still waiting. I'm on edge.

Then the light of the sun, rising, flashes in my face — I inhale the sharp odour of light on wet.

Eventually, I've walked so far that the hotel is a dark speck against the distant woods.

Soon I hear water and see that I've come to a stream — or small river — with steep reddish banks, and a footbridge which looks narrow but perfectly sturdy, as if it's in regular use. The sky's a chill yellow, and bird song is deafening now, as dawn begins to happen. The air's sharp and cold. I pull my hands inside the cuffs of my jumper.

I walk on to the centre of this bridge and look down.

The water's moving deep and fast, pulling at grass and twigs as it drags and foams along the banks on either side. It's hard to tell how deep it is — six foot, maybe, at the deepest point.

No one knows where I am.

I do not wonder why I've come, why I'm here. I know that I could go in there, easy as pie — just lose my grip, my breath, and by the time I panicked it would be too late and the rest would be quick, surreptitious. There would be a moment of terror – oh yes, of course, I don't deny it – but it would be brief, wouldn't it, and soon I wouldn't know? There'd be no choice – the water wouldn't relent and my body would be dragged down so fast – I'm attracted to that. I'm still exhilarated at having come this far, at having found this place. I'm less afraid and more certain than I've ever been. I could deal with my pain so quickly, control it. No one would lose out.

Hypnotized by the height and the quick movement underneath, I test the handrail gently with my weight.

'Well, before you go any further, do you want to talk about it?' Alistair's voice. I don't look around. I let him interrupt, as he must, though it's not fair of course. He doesn't know anything.

'About what?' I must admit, I'm impatient, cagey. 'How do you know what I'm going to do?' How can he know if I don't?

'How can I know?' he comes back at me. 'If you'll never talk?'

'But it's you,' I cry, noticing the blackness in the water, tears starting into my eyes, 'it's you who won't talk to me. You think I don't try, but I do – I do at least sometimes try.'

'You don't really like me,' he says, 'you never did, not really. At first, it wasn't your fault – I encouraged you. I wanted you, whatever, and I thought you probably did love me. But after that, you pretended. And if Jack had never existed . . .' He sighs. 'You make me sad. Save yourself the trouble. I know you. It's not what you're going to do, so don't pretend, Susan.'

Well, we'll see who's pretending. We'll see who knows what. I squat down on the bridge, gripping the damp wooden handrail above me, resting my head on my wrists. The water rushes past, black and tempting, sending a spray of bubbles toward the bank. Such a sweet and simple thing to do, not awful at all, as I'd expected. Easy and sweet – natural, even. I notice, now, that my hands are really wet.

'You'd never do it,' says Jack, certain and content, and I lift my head with surprise and see that he's almost grown up and that he turned out tall and good and wonderful, just as I always hoped and knew he would.

'Oh,' I say, tears springing into my eyes simply because it's him, because my whole body, heart and limbs, jumps into space at the sound of his voice, 'you stayed dark, like your baby hair – and quite curly, oh I'm so glad!'

I gulp, gobble him up, take him all in – after all, this might not come again. I might need this. I need to know what happened, how he ended up – I want to press my face into his, feel the breadth of his shoulders, tell him things, show him photos of when he was a baby, measure my love and hold it up.

'You'd never do it,' he continues, and his chin is just as I'd thought, clever and certain, 'because I need my milk.'

'Ah,' I say, quick and bitter – and sorry about it even as

I speak — 'ah, milk — is that all? But when that's finished, when that's gone?' He reaches out with his hand and I could kiss the strong thumb, the long straight male fingers. He is so grown, so full and strong. I made him.

'We did, Susan, we, not just you,' Alistair says, but — without looking — I know that he's already walking away, fading with the darkness, blurring into the watery brilliance of dawn. I turn quickly, to check Jack's still there. He is.

'Well, then there will be something else,' he continues, 'you know it's more than milk. And after that something else — something else that's mine, that isn't yours to take. We both know it. We know you'd never go.'

I can't speak any more. I want him so much.

Jack looks at me for a moment, a matter-of-fact son's smile on his face. I thought he was grown-up, but now I notice that he can't be, the curves of his face slide so easily into one another, so perfect and soft. He slips his thumb in his mouth and then I don't really think he's gone, but I can't look, can't see him.

My belly contracts, my breasts ache. I must get back to the hotel, before he wakes.

Some insect is skimming over the surface of the water. I'm so still that each blade of grass now has its own separate violent movement. The water's silver, the sky bright with the possibility of sunshine.

As I start the long walk back to the hotel, only two things are clear to me: that this long dialogue with myself is practically over; and that I'll leave Alistair — no matter how much time it takes me, no matter how much it hurts the three of us.

In retrospect, there's something fluid and perfect about my dream, something ultimately comforting – as if it's been happening all along, all this time, without a gap, unknown to me.

I'm moving, soundless, through a large house I've never seen before – tiled hall, sweeping staircase, long landing. It is night. I glance out of the window at the greenish moonlit lawn, at the dark lily pond where a heron used to come, at the terrace where George sat while he was dying, at the spot, now thick with bracken, weeds, and rusting metal, where Queenie burned his things. I see without surprise that she's sitting out there in the sour, cold glare of the moon, in the night, on her slatted chaise longue, smiling. Her face is younger, happier.

'Oh, Susan,' she smiles, and her voice is far away and liquid, the ends of words fading into one another, 'we've all been dead so long. More than thirty years . . . so lonely. Whatever kept you?'

As I walk through the house, the night thickens around me, pulling me closer to its heart – I can hardly make out furniture, objects, where this armchair or table begins, where fabric, glass, leather end. I know where to go, I'm welcomed in. The house sighs, breathes, relaxes to accommodate me. Clocks tick, water races through the pipes.

I know where to look. I know I'll find him at last, on the top landing, near the maid's room, shivering and staring into space. His arms extended in front of him, and there are tears still frozen on his cheeks. There isn't much time.

'Come on,' I say, softly, careful not to wake him, 'come on, I'll take you back to bed now . . .' And I encircle his small cold body with my arms and lift him, and sniff his head and the inch of soft flesh behind his ears. And he smells of my Jack — of small boy's hair and warm creases and bare soles of feet and fingers. I hold him for a moment, and realize what I've known all along: that this is it — this is all there is — just Jack, and other little boys, and my poor, poor father, who had no love.

In his room, the curtain blows out and a splash of moonlight shows me one side of his face. From his bed, we can see that Queenie is still there on the lawn, her back to us.

'I love you, Susan,' he says, as I tuck him back in to the bed, pulling sheets and blankets and eiderdown up over his little, shivery form. 'Will you ever forgive me?' and in the dream, my face is suddenly a curtain of tears, and I lay it down beside his on the pillow — not wanting to leave him as I know I must, wanting to be close and still and silent for a while longer.

Then it's over, and I wake.

When I look around the bedroom, I realize the peculiar

noticeable silence is in fact peace. Alistair breathes beside me, mouth open, one arm extended above his head. I prop myself on my elbow and look into the grey half-light and know straight away that I'll never see him again, that something's gone, a shadow's lifted, relinquished its hold. The wall seems to smile.

And then finally, gratefully, I begin to cry.

seven

'It is difficult and unwise to wake a sleepwalker, particularly a child. It may cause distress or even hysteria. It is best simply to guide them gently back to bed.'

Queenie went into a nursing home in the spring of 1980, even though Douglas had promised her many times that she wouldn't have to. But one day she just woke up and realized her things had been packed around her, and he drove her over there with the music turned up loud on his car radio, leaving her with a cup of tea going cold and the evening paper.

She was well over eighty. She'd been managing perfectly well up until then, but from the moment she entered the home she became very unsteady on her legs and began to wet the bed occasionally (well, let them clear it up, she thought, they're paid to do it), but her mind was otherwise clear as crystal, always had been.

At first Douglas visited her twice a week, but this was quickly pared down to once, on a Friday evening, switching on the TV as soon as he arrived. She persuaded herself that she did not mind, adjusting her expectations, feeding off his presence in the room, just the sound of his breathing, the click of his lighter, the occasional remark which came her way, which she caught (she didn't bother with her hearing aid these days – there seemed to be no point). But soon he came less and less, until one day she realized it must be almost three weeks and he'd not phoned or anything. She lay there, the insides of her thighs cold and sticky with pee, and tried not to panic. She asked the nurse to try and reach him on the phone, to say she was ill – anything – but the nurse looked embarrassed and bit her lip and explained that he'd told her he was very busy at work and would come as soon as he could.

More time passed, minutes, days, she didn't know. She lay and watched the wall of her room. She saw no point in easing herself out of bed to sit by the window. Every time she moved, the plastic undersheet crackled. On the Formica bedside table, beside the plastic water jug, she kept an old Polaroid photograph of her grandchildren – Susan, Sara, and Penny – which the nurses often admired, trying to goad her into conversation. She hadn't set eyes on them or spoken to them of course since Douglas ceased contact all those years ago.

She didn't really know why she'd kept the photo – a silly whim – yet it was surprising how often she stared at those little faces and willed them to speak to her.

'Well, good morning, Mrs Hancock – how are we today?' the nurse said one insignificant bright morning, placing a Tupperware container of pills on the table. Queenie did not respond or move. She felt no pain, no struggle, but it was as if someone lay on top of her (was it George, trying to press his silly hardness into her all over again?), forcing her down into a well of darkness. A bell rang three times. It sounded like music.

'Can we have some help here, quickly please . . .' was the last thing she heard before something slipped, and the dark was total.

None of us have had any contact with Penny for several months.

Then she rings Mummy on her birthday and invites her out to dinner at a restaurant in Covent Garden. Over dinner, she shows her photos of her holidays in New York and Paris, and tells her she's bought a penthouse flat on the river at Kew. She's given up her job and split up with her boyfriend. She's going to take some time off; she needs space and time. She says she still finds the loss of her father hard to bear. She's emotionally fragile. She's thinking of seeing a psychiatrist.

'It's a terrible thing he did to her,' says Mummy, after-wards, and I force myself to remember that this is her baby, her Jack, she's talking about, 'a terrible legacy he passed on . . . she's very lonely, you know. What really gave me the creeps was that she was wearing all those great ugly rings of Queenie's – they looked so odd on her, forced and grotesque, like a little girl dressing up. They're ghastly but I suppose the truth is they must be worth a fortune.'

*

Spring arrives properly, hot and bright.

Jack sleeps, magically, through the night, and this continues until I begin to wake every day feeling calm and revived. I phone Mr Sudbury and tell him I'll come back to work, part-time, in a fortnight.

I throw my head and heart back into my painting and produce four large canvases: three of them are soft, bright, abstract oils. Colours thrown on top of one another, easy, generous squares of cobalt blue and yellow and leaf green, shot with white. The fourth is of Jack — halfway between waking and sleeping, his bottom hunched in the air, his fists straight out in front — on the blue-violet counterpane of our bed. After a small amount of nerve and effort, I get the first three exhibited in a new gallery in Battersea and — to my astonishment — they're all sold within a week. I can see Alistair is impressed, by the absorbed and expert way in which he scrutinizes the cheque. The one of Jack I give to my mother.

One day when I'm feeling particularly lithe and grown-up, I get my hair cut, blunt and shiny, and parade stark naked to myself in front of my long bedroom mirror. Someone I hardly know any more stares back at me.

I no longer dream about my father, or see ghosts. In fact, I don't dream at all.

Ede is married early in May.

She insists that it will be small — just immediate family

and friends – but of course Ede couldn't do anything even slightly small.

Grown-up laughter in a huge gothic sunlit room; brunch and beautiful hats, and people leaning towards one another, kissing, touching. Jazz from a live band. Through the arched doorways, flung wide on to the garden, pale thick pear blossom and the beginnings of a heat wave. Julian so off-puttingly attractive that he gives the impression of being cold and unapproachable, which Ede has already assured me he is not, and Ede herself, made of sunshine, her make up softened by her frequent tears, pushing a fork through a plate of kedgeree.

Alistair holds Jack, four months old, who dribbles happily all over his best suit. I watch them from across the room where they're surrounded by women who clearly think they're cute together. Yes, I think, he's a perfectly sweet father, tender and proud, just the smallest bit hassled about his suit, but determined not to be, insisting to himself that it doesn't matter – that a dry-cleaning bill is only a dry-cleaning bill after all. Objectively, if I pretend to look at him as if for the first time, from over here, I am pleased with what I see – impressed all over again.

Lenny's standing at the foot of the big ornate staircase with his new girlfriend, Karen. She's a sculptor – serious, thin, beautiful in a flawed and interesting way, dressed entirely in black. Girlfriend is my word. He insists they're just friends, that they don't sleep together (and who knows? that may even be true) but I can see from the way she leans towards him and faces out into the room from that specific vantage point, that this is entirely academic; it's only a matter of time. Somewhere in my head, or body – I don't know – this hurts. The thought of his arms, of our sex, the smell of his face, still gives me pain. But it has nothing to do with love, I tell myself.

A few weeks ago, when he'd more or less accepted that our thing was over, he called me at the clinic:

'Look, I have this friend, Karen.'

'Well?'

'I don't love her, there's nothing between us. We're friends. She's good – you'd like her . . .'

'Lenny' – very sad, very patient – 'why are you telling me this?'

'I just wanted you to know. In case you come across her, or something.' Something?

Now he looks straight at me and I smile and shrug, what else can I do? Then, keeping his eyes on me, he pats Karen on the arm and breaks away from the group and comes over. We move, with our champagne glasses, over to a knobbly old-fashioned radiator.

'Are you OK?' he asks, looking into my eyes, then at my mouth, chin, hands. 'How's Jack?'

I know straight away that he's slightly drunk.

'He's fine. We're all fine.'

'Good.' He looks away, looks all around the room, then, 'Oh Susan,' he says, extending a long finger to touch my wrist, 'you really are something. You know that.'

'Well,' I say, and look around the room also. Alistair notices, winks at me, touches Jack's head with his chin, 'well, you're drunk. But it doesn't matter.'

This is an example of something, I think, I could learn from this. But the idea dissolves before I've managed to think it.

'I love you,' he continues, 'you do realize there's no one else?' I smile. Despite everything, I smile. 'I'm drunk,' he adds, glancing in Karen's direction. She pretends not to notice. He looks unbearably young, fragile, a lost boy. Again, the sight of him up close is terrible to me, painful. 'I love you,' he says again, more unhappily this time.

'Look, I'm trying to sort myself out,' I say.

Thank God I finished it, I think, thank God Alistair never found out. Even if I leave him (and really, I think I will), I don't want it to be like that − I don't want him to know what I did. Then I remember Lenny in his long black coat in the frozen park, and my heart begins involuntarily to snag, the beginnings of a tear along a weak spot.

'I'm fine,' I say, gripping the warm stem of my glass, 'it's all for the best. Really, Lenny.'

Still he looks at me and his eyes are doing that thing, pinning my shoulders somehow, prising my limbs apart, heating something in my solar plexus. The beautiful but flawed girl in black is now looking at us; we're pausing, looking down too much.

'She looks nice,' I add with conviction, certain that what I must do is drive him away, 'she looks interesting.'

'Oh, Susan.'

And he looks at me, and I just look away. A perfectly controlled act.

And already now when I look back he's gone, moving away from me, walking over to the staircase where Karen claims him with a hand. I stare for a second at the space where he was – it's still imprinted, somehow still holds the edges of his shape.

And, though whole seconds pass – or a flow of days and nights – and really I'm as good as alone in that room full of ghosts and unfinished things, I know exactly what will happen next.

What will happen is I'll be standing there by the radiator, dry eyed, frozen with the effort, remembering how a particular passion felt. And Al will come over and hold you out to me because his arms are aching and it's my turn. And I'll kiss your warm, damp neck and we'll make our way out through the people and the music, past Ede who smiles and tries to tell us something – out into the hot bright garden, where together we'll look at the lilies and the big red fish and, finally, I'll sit and feed you in the shade.

Or maybe not. Maybe I'll just sit down with you, right there in the middle of everything, exactly where I am, glad for a reason to stop.

'Sweetheart,' I'll whisper, 'sweetheart' – my arms filled up, my head still dark and undecided.